Praise for

"In Laura Carpini's beautifully c̣ı̣ treated to a multi-dimensional journey into a shamanic ıaıı̣uɔ̣ɔ̣ɔ̣ɔ̣. Wisdom infuses every page. Innocence, its loss and recovery, leads the reader through difficult terrain into redemption. In *Bear Speaks*, Ms. Carpini has both channeled as well as orchestrated a fable for our times. Every encounter with the wild world is magical. This is a lovely, essential book that belongs among the few possessions every pilgrim carries on the road to self-discovery." —GARY LEMONS, poet, author of *Fresh Horses*

"A charming story that shows us how to conquer fear to find a life of joy. *Bear Speaks* is not only an engaging story, it is filled with wonderful lessons about living life to its fullest." —SANDRA INGERMAN, author of *How to Thrive in Changing Times*

"*Bear Speaks* is rich with the feeling of uncovering the truth of Self. It captivates the mind and teaches us to uncover the joy in modern life. I wholeheartedly recommend it." —ERICH SCHIFFMANN, author of *Yoga: The Spirit and Practice of Moving into Stillness*

"We all seek a light to live by. We might discover a bit of truth in a colorful shell, a bit of wisdom in our backyard. And every so often, there is a book not only worth seeking out, but one that seeks us out. *Bear Speaks* is such a book. I had tears in my eyes at its conclusion, not because I was sorrowful, but joyful. Who would have guessed that a bear would serve as the unlikely narrator of practical explanations of immortal wisdom? I am grateful it has sought me out, to teach me and light my own life." —CYNDI DALE, author of *The Subtle Body*

"Laura Carpini's *Bear Speaks* tells an enchanting tale about trusting what presents itself to us in life and conquering our fears to find the world of joy and fulfillment. —LYNN ANDREWS, *New York Times* and internationally best-selling author of the Medicine Woman series

Bear Speaks

The Story of
7 Sacred Lessons
Learned from a
Montana Grizzly

Laura Carpini

WEISER BOOKS
San Francisco, CA / Newburyport, MA

First published in 2010 by
Red Wheel/Weiser, LLC
With offices at:
500 Third Street, Suite 230
San Francisco, CA 94107
www.redwheelweiser.com

Copyright © 2010 by Laura Carpini
All rights reserved. No part of this publication may be reproduced or transmitted in any form
or by any means, electronic or mechanical, including photocopying, recording, or by any
information storage and retrieval system, without permission in writing from Red Wheel/
Weiser, LLC. Reviewers may quote brief passages.

ISBN: 978-1-57863-482-8

Library of Congress Cataloging-in-Publication Data is available on request.

Cover and text design by Maxine Ressler
Typeset in Fournier
Cover photograph © Adrienne Miller/iStockphoto.com
Cover painting by Pat Olchefski-Winston

Printed in the United States of America
TS

10 9 8 7 6 5 4 3 2 1

The paper used in this publication meets the minimum requirements of the American National
Standard for Information Sciences—Permanence of Paper for Printed Library Materials
Z39.48-1992 (R1997).

Disclaimer

THIS BOOK IS INSPIRED BY the author's experiences camping at Feathered Pipe Ranch in Helena, Montana. It is, however, a work of fiction. Any character's resemblance to persons alive or dead is purely coincidental.

Dedication

To my grandmother, Rose Paraglia Carpini
I am learning from her even now.

Acknowledgments

I AM INDEBTED TO MY editor, Caroline Pincus, for seeing the value in the story that was to become *Bear Speaks*, and for having the patience and courage to get it published. Her comments, along with those of associate managing editor Rachel Leach and copy-editor Ali McCort, resulted in a more coherent telling of the story. Thanks also to Lisa Trudeau, Bonni Hamilton, Susie Pitzen and everyone at Red Wheel/Weiser.

Thanks to Erich Schiffmann for his encouragement and cheer-leading. He listened with patience, understanding, and acceptance, giving me the impetus to write my ideas on paper.

To Anne Jablonski and poet Gary Lemons: thank you for moti-vating me to turn *Bear Speaks* from a conversation piece into a completed book. I thank all the yogis who gather in classes and at home, and who meet every year at Feathered Pipe Ranch to practice. Feathered Pipe is a unique place of retreat. I thank India Supera for her wisdom in keeping it open and running for all of us to enjoy.

I can't extend enough thanks to artist Pat Olchefski-Winston for painting the image of the Grizzly. Thanks to Donna Linden and the art department at Red Wheel/Weiser for taking care that her work was reproduced properly for the cover.

To my support group of friends, particularly Monika McCar-thy, Mike Edwards, Bonnie Delight, Duke McDaniel, Ramona Pal, Abby Burton, Andrea Eisen, Wendi Papo, Julie Matheson, and Bill and June Wolff: thank you for all of it.

I thank the teachers, administrators, and staff of the Redondo Beach Unified School District for granting me the time to write, and for inspiring me on a daily basis. To all my students who are really my teachers, it's been wonderful getting to talk about books and write with you.

Love and gratitude to both my parents. They've encouraged me to strike out as my own person from the first, gifted me with a sense of passion, and taught me to appreciate life. I thank my brother Chase for his humor and helpfulness.

Thank you to Mary Shaffer, my aunt and confidant. She was there at the beginning, making sure I was warm, comfortable and dry. True to form, she sat with me for hours the night I completed the first draft, listening to what was to become Bear Speaks with enthusiasm.

I thank Layton Pace for being my husband. He offered love and support during the time it took to put this book together, anchoring our family in the most significant of ways.

Finally, to my daughter, Anne Monique: you are anything but typical. Your ability to hear the music for what it is has been invaluable, and yes, your smile really does remind me over and over again that it is possible to love without limit.

Contents

Camping Alone

I CAN'T FULLY EXPLAIN MY need to be alone, only that those closest to me are driving me crazy: my father and his repeated insistence that I get a real job; mom, with her constant worries about my well-being as a single woman living in an "edgy" part of Torrance, California, near Los Angeles; and Brian with his hurt looks and constant pressure to book a wedding ceremony in churches of which we are not, and never will be, members.

My father is a self-made businessman with dreams of his only child rising to prominence as a stockbroker. I struggled through a business degree, but now I teach high school math. Needless to say, Dad is not pleased.

The most contentment in my twenty-five years comes from my relationship with Brian, the supposed love of my life. He proposed last year. I accepted the ring. The problem is I can't commit to the actual wedding. Just thinking about it gives me hives—literally. Brian is also disappointed.

I've camped a couple times, so I know the basics. Dad's taught me to put up a tent. He's shown me how to thread poles through the tent loops to make it stand upright, and how to filter water from potentially germ-infested streams. I borrow his tent, water pump, camping stove, and down sleeping bag. I roll them all up and attach them to my twice-used backpack.

By the time I board the junket plane for Helena, everyone—the screaming children, the polished businesspeople on their cell phones, the short-tempered security workers herding us through metal detectors—is an annoyance. I lease a car for the month from a nearly deserted dirt lot and drive away with gleeful superiority.

Northern Montana is rough and inaccessible, as far away from Los Angeles as I can afford. I tell Brian and my folks that they can find me in the Helena National Forest, home of several Native American tribes, including the Blackfoot Indian Tribe. This potential isolation puts my mother in a dither. I promise to keep my cell phone on at all times, but neglect to mention there is probably no reception.

In five minutes I am at the local market, which is staffed by Jerry, a helpful gentleman in overalls with salt-and-pepper gray hair. He looks as if he can fix anything. He proves it by unclogging the toilet in the back before advising me on camping locations and supplies.

"There's an abandoned lodge with campsites bordering the edge of the forest there," he informs me. "I've been clearing trails there for the Forest Service for twenty years." He unrolls a topographic map on the counter. I point to the most remote section on it I can find.

"I want somewhere with no people," I specify.

Jerry raises an eyebrow. I suppose with my thick eyeglasses and gangly frame I don't look like the type of person who camps out in the woods alone. Jerry explains that there is an abandoned retreat house in the forest there. "It's been closed for years now. Campsites are still available to the public. Private, if that's what you want."

I plop fifteen dollars down on the counter for the camping permit. Jerry hesitates. "Honey, you know it's the height of summer."

"But you just said—"

"I can't promise you'll be entirely alone out there."

I push the money toward him, decided. I also purchase the map, cookware, numerous cans of baked beans, lunch meat, bread, sunscreen, a flashlight, and a lantern.

After we pack my gear into the trunk, Jerry circles my chosen spot on the map with a yellow highlighter, directing me to head north on the main road about five miles, then make a sharp left down an undeveloped dirt road for another two miles into the area. I wave goodbye as he calls out one final bit of advice: watch for bears. Black ones are swarming the place this summer.

A piney smell assaults my nostrils the moment I open the car door at the end of the dirt road. Alder and maple trees mix with various species of pines; the varying shades of green extend some fifty feet over my head. Despite the density of those trees, an intensely blue sky dominates the space up there.

I drag my backpack along the dusty trail about a mile, following Jerry's highlighted path on the map. A smaller path veers off to the right where I discover the log-slatted lodge. It sits next to the lake, grand in its position snuggled between two snow-topped mountains.

As promised, the place is deserted. A sign on the side door reads: NO SHOES BEYOND THIS POINT. I drop my pack, slip off my shoes, and turn the knob. The door slides open easily.

"Hello?" My voice echoes back at me from the empty building.

I wander inside a large meeting room where a giant elk head stares down at me from above an oversized fireplace. His eyes are soft and knowing. At least someone knows where I am, I think.

I poke through the empty side rooms and back out to my waiting backpack. After trudging another mile down the main path, I discover the bath house. I am relieved that when I turn the knob to one of the showers, hot water gushes out. There is also a comfortable-looking sauna that makes a steamy, fizzing noise when I hit the "on" button. I turn it off, planning to return later.

The campsites are yet another mile or so down the path. I choose one by a creek. It makes a lovely gurgling noise as it tinkles over rocks into the lake.

It takes me two full hours and five trips back down the path to transfer everything from the car over to the campsite. By the time I finish, I am dusty, hot, and thirsty. I slurp down water from a plastic bottle before tackling the tent. Inserting the metal poles into the flaps correctly turns out to be the trial of my day. They tend to buckle when I attempt to thread them into the tent flaps. Only after a full hour of painstaking threading with the side poles do I realize that I need to thread the larger poles through the top of the tent first in order for it to stand upright. I yank the side poles out again, cursing as they repeatedly buckle during the process. It takes me another hour to secure the spikes into the ground by stomping on them with my boots. By the time the tent is erect and ready for business, the sun sets.

After an equally frustrating struggle with my camping stove, it ignites, and I manage to heat a can of beans. I sop them up with pieces of the bread, hungrier than I've felt in years. It is dark when I finally zip up the door to the tent, turn off my lantern, and crawl into the waiting sleeping bag. I remove my glasses, placing them safely on the floor of the tent next to my head. Yet the more I pretend to relax, the more sleep becomes an impossibility. Strange noises engulf the tent. I hear the flap of a bird's wings above me, then a loud *Whoo hoo! Whoo hoo!*—maybe an owl.

Next comes a curious shuffling sound from the nearby foliage—soft and tentative, clearly some ground animal—a squirrel or a raccoon, I posit. I turn over in my sleeping bag, determined to remain nonplussed.

The wind increases until it whips relentlessly through the alder trees. Odd chattering sounds echo from the trees with increased volume until finally I hear the rustling of something large outside my tent; its hooves thud heavily through the pine needles.

I sit straight up and light the lantern. Okay, that was probably just a deer. The thudding hooves sound like they're right next to the tent. Deer never attack humans, do they? Nah, I tell myself, that's impossible. I'm only imagining that this deer or whatever it is with the hooves is that close. Then I hear a loud brushing noise as it rubs its body against the other side of the tent. So it is that close. I feel woozy.

What am I doing here? I love Los Angeles. It's a city full of people, restaurants, shops, and opportunities. My friends and family live there. If something attacks me in my Torrance apartment, I have only to pick up the phone and dial 911. Out here there isn't even any cell service.

I listen as the hooves prance away into the night. I'm okay for now, I tell myself as I snuggle back into the bag. Besides, in the morning I can pack up and fly back to L.A. That's it, I think, I just need to relax, get through this one night. I'll book a flight home tomorrow.

But the longer I lie here, alert, tense, wide awake, the more relaxation becomes a joke. The hooves return, and the undefined animal clattering is joined by rustling in the bushes and the increasing sound of a stronger and stronger wind. My tent rattles. My thoughts spin over and over again, reeling repeatedly through my restless mind: Brian down on one knee, pressuring me to marry, my father reprimanding me for forgetting the correct way to thread tent poles, overly aggressive deer kicking down my tent, snapping at me with large, unnatural teeth. That's it—I'm about to be attacked by a battalion of mutant forest animals, all out for human blood. I don't actually fall asleep until near dawn, and that is only after I grope through my backpack for a sleeping pill, choking it down in an attempt to silence the escalating racket in my mind.

When I wake, it is the middle of the day. My body feels stiff and overwrought. I discover a mysterious sticky substance, probably pitch, on the corner of the right lens of my glasses. After an unsuccessful attempt to rub it away with bottled water and the bottom of my T-shirt, I give up and slide the glasses onto my nose. The sap-like globs on the right side of the lens cloud my vision.

The forest, so frenetic the night before, seems sedate now, soft, like the filtered sunlight through the canopy of pine trees. I find myself surrounded by bird sounds—twittering, chirping, and eventually a steady tapping against the tree near my tent. When I unzip the door and stick my head outside, I catch sight of a woodpecker. He pauses at the appearance of my head, and then dives for the crumbs from my dinner last night. I watch as he and his less colorful mate deliver the crumbs to a nest at the side of the tree.

I've never actually seen a woodpecker's nest before. Slowly I exit the tent in time to watch the tops of five small beaks open simultaneously into one giant, hungry gape. The parents drop my crumbs inside the waiting mouths.

I put a pot of water on the camp stove, pick a pine needle from my hair before pulling it into a ponytail, and unfurl the map onto a log next to the tent. Jerry did mention he worked on some of these trails for the Forest Service, and I am itching to explore them. Any thoughts of leaving the forest for the safety of the city dissolve with the grains of instant coffee I stir into my cup of boiling water.

I hike Jerry's groomed trails, packing a lunch to eat by the lake. The same *whoo hoo* cry from the night before follows me. I look up to see not an owl, but a raven, large, black, and formidable over my head; she circles above, heralding me and every other creature in the woods with her intermittent *whoo hoo*. Each time, it sends a shiver of expectation through my being.

After lunch, I sit on the wood dock that stretches over the lake. I take the spiral notebook from my day pack, and begin.

• *June 21, 2008*

Hello Diary.

I'm a mathematician, not a writer, so please excuse the lousy prose. I need to speak with someone. It's about my father. He's been sick the past month with cancer of the esophagus. Whoever heard of that? I figure I'm responsible somehow. Maybe by letting him down, I've weakened his immune system.

I toss the notebook down on the grass in disgust. How stupid is this, me keeping a diary? I don't want to write down feelings. I know: I'll just record the facts every day. Stick to what actually happens.

OVER THE NEXT WEEK, I fall into a routine. Each night, the forest becomes unbearably alive. The unidentified hooves and the wind kick in around midnight, growing in intensity, shaking the sides of my tent over and over again until around dawn, when I succumb to frustrated exhaustion and drug myself to sleep.

I wake around ten to the filtered sunlight and the sound of the woodpecker family rustling together their breakfast. I gulp large quantities of instant coffee before stumbling over to the bath house for a shower followed by a sauna.

Back at the tent, I pack myself a peanut butter and jelly sandwich for lunch, grab the map, and explore nearby trails, always ending my hike on the lawn in front of the lake. I hold my journal and a pen, consider that I might record the events of the day, but push the pages aside and opt for a nap instead. Dinner is either baked beans or pasta with a slice of bread.

After eating, I trudge back over to the bath house to rinse the cookware. I am not such a green camper as to miss the importance of putting away food at night. All sorts of critters could come right into my campsite, right into the tent, even, if I were to entice them with food. I remember my father telling me that wild animals are frightened by humans. I realize they would quickly push that fear aside if they were hungry enough.

The evening always climaxes with vows on my part to pack and return to Los Angeles in the morning. Then, I knock myself into oblivion with a sleeping pill.

• June 26, 2008

Why am I even out here? I want to leave this place, yet on some level, I have to admit it excites me.

Now that sounds really dumb. It makes no sense for me to stay here, putting my life on hold to sit up with insomnia night after night.

Maybe I'll just camp a little longer, just a couple more nights, and see what happens. What could be the harm in that?

• June 27, 2008

I know I'm breaking my own rule here, the no feelings in the journal thing, but oh well. I keep thinking about Brian.

I want to love him. It seems right that I should love him. I'm twenty-five; isn't that when people are supposed to fall in love and get married? But there's something counter to "should" out here in the woods, something about the empty sky that compels me to break rules. I like the feeling of freedom out here.

Maybe I want to be empty in the end, like that sky—empty and free. I'm trying to dig to this deeper level, and maybe the answer is there's nothing deeper to find, that it's all just surface anyway. Marriage is sort of a solution to that emptiness, isn't it? Institutionalized togetherness—marriage and then children. I mean, it's safe; you know what you're getting when you sign up for that. Crap, now I sound like my mother.

I doubt if marriage is much of a guarantee anyway. It's not like I've done a stellar job connecting with my own parents. I bet Dad wishes he had a son, someone with more backbone. I haven't invented anything. I haven't made a million dollars. I probably even stink at teaching math. I'm certainly not self-sufficient like he always wanted me to be. I'm still borrowing money to pay my

8

rent. My wardrobe is the result of an overzealous use of credit cards. I bet dad has to make an effort to feign happiness with me—his only child.

I stop writing. There is something off about this place—this forest, this lodge, this lake. It's not normal. I'm completely alone here, logically I know that, but I feel like something or someone is watching me right now.

That notion feels incredibly creepy. My pulse goes up at the thought of it—this undisclosed being, spying from who knows where, behind the pine trees maybe, or inside the lodge.

There is a charge to the idea, an edgy feeling. Awareness of this *other* comes from somewhere beyond my five usual senses; it jostles a powerful, heretofore unrealized, connector in my mind.

And it hits all at once.

• *June 28, 2008*

Someone was definitely watching me as I shuffled through the woods today. I am being stalked.

• *June 29, 2008*

I sense the stalker more and more. He watches me roll my sleeping bag each night in my tent. He sees me drive into Helena for the cans of baked beans that have become a staple. I find myself looking for him behind me as I hike.

I am free of him at the market or local gas station, but such respites from my spy are rare, mainly because I go into town less and less now. It's too easy to stock up on necessities in one shot, gives me more time alone out here. I've grown attached to the unadulterated quiet here in the woods. I've never been so aware of my own thoughts before. But I'm not alone because of the mysterious Presence.

The Presence crouches around trees; it envelops me no matter where I walk. Of course, this sense of being constantly watched could be a figment of my imagination. Maybe I'm inventing this fictional someone out of boredom.

I should really get out of here. This place is doing a number on my head.

• July 1, 2008

The Presence is always there—always. Maybe he's a spirit, or a phantom who watches my movements from above, never actually making contact. My personal phantom.

• July 2, 2008

Look, I know I'm a selfish girl. I'm not sure why I'm here. I suspect somewhere in these woods, the Presence holds the answer. He knows me.

While I'm sitting here writing like this, or squirming in the tent at night, I'm exposed. Anything could rip through those fragile flaps that divide me from the forest. Maybe I deserve that. Maybe on some level I'm inviting it.

Hey, you out there, can you read these words? Come get me. I know you're there. Whenever I feel you watch me, I get this adrenaline rush. It's like rock climbing without a rope, being out here with you. Not that I've ever been rock climbing. Jesus, my life's been dull until now.

I like you. I like the sense of danger attached to you, and that's why I'm letting you see everything when you watch. Who are you?

I put down the pages and watch the sun as it reflects off the surface of the lake. What's wrong with me? If there really is someone out there, stalking me, I should be terrified. He could be anybody: a purse snatcher, a rapist, an ax murderer. I stand, stretch up on tiptoe, and raise my arms to the empty sky.

I know he's not an ax murderer.

• *July 4, 2008*

I heard him breathe today. His breath was steady, slow, and even. It followed me with unnerving regularity on my hike this morning. The sound of it got louder and louder with each step.

Now I can't hear anything. Where did it go? I'm feeling . . . oddly rejected by its disappearance. Maybe whatever it is went away forever.

I walk the path to the rental car, turn on the motor, and drive as calmly as I can down the hill into Helena. I park in the lot by Jerry's camping store, pull my cell phone from my pocket, and dial Brian's number. The steady ringing of the phone is followed by his wooden voice on the answering machine.

I cough, clear my head before speaking. "Hey, honey, it's me. Hanging out here in the woods. Just wanted to hear your voice. I'm fine. I'll call tomorrow. You know I love you."

When I look out the window, I see Jerry, watching me tentatively from the doorway of the store. I don't want to talk to Jerry right now.

He waves. I roll down the window.

"Everything okay?" Jerry calls.

"Oh, yeah. I was just making a phone call." I turn the key in the ignition, back out of the lot.

I'm losing my mind. Only a crazy person acts like this.

I FEEL MORE RESTLESS THAN usual as I prepare for nightfall. I pace the campsite, secure the metal spikes holding my tent into the ground. The wind picks up early, before I even finish my baked beans. I crawl into the tent as soon as it gets dark and take my sleeping pill early. It is the last one in the container.

I wake up in the middle of the night to the sound of breathing all around me, a distinct sucking in and out that reverberates through my tent. I realize with fascination that whatever it is, it is breathing just outside, right next to my head.

The breath is loud. The breath is sensuous. It is terrifying and unavoidable, the in-out, out-in rhythm of it. I know by its beat that it is attached to a living heart, full of unrequited yearning for connection, just as surely as my own heart yearns and aches there in the dark.

I shudder at the breathing, but in the same instant, smile. That thing that stalks me with undeniable certainty has found me at last. The sound, my sound, is real and loud and imminent. Despite my fear, I am relieved.

I consider exiting the tent to confront whoever or whatever is out there. Instead I curl deeper into the sleeping bag and listen to his breathing.

• *July 7, 2008*

It's been several days since I heard him at my tent, and nothing's happened: no breathing, no sense of someone watching me from the bushes, nothing. I've been hiking the forest along the usual paths every morning, ready for I know not what.

Last night, I searched for the source of the breath with a flashlight under every twig and rock. It's so frustrating. I know something was there, but now there's nothing, nothing, nothing. I feel completely alone.

• *July 8, 2008*

Today I came eye to eye with a Doe and her twin fawns. So stunning was she, so charming her offspring, that for a moment I forgot the mysterious breath.

I wondered if the source of the breathing was the Doe, but realized this is impossible. The Breather was undeniably male; I sense this fact. I bet he even lurked about the forest somewhere quite close then, watching me watch the Doe. As I gazed at the mother and her twins in awe, I sensed his presence.

• *July 8, 2008 (Evening)*

I'm finding it difficult to put down the journal tonight. So I'm breaking my established routine to get back to it.

The light of the lantern tonight makes it easy to write sitting outside the tent on a log. That way I can look up every once in a while at the stars. Were my father here, he would be able to name all the constellations in that northern summer sky. As it is, I can pick out some of them myself: Cassiopeia, Orion's belt, and far off in the distance, traces of the curve of lights that compose the Milky Way. The sleeping bag wrapped tightly around my body feels warm and cozy.

• *July 8, 2008 (Later)*

My heart fills with an indescribable yearning, a conscious need to find the Source, the he who watches me always. I have experienced this type of longing before on many occasions; I have often squelched it with alcohol, sex, even food back in Los Angeles. Here, there is nothing with which to squelch the need, so

*I am left with it, raw, circumspect; what I feel now can only be
described as an ache.*

*I should learn to meditate. I like the idea of it—clearing my
cluttered mind of all that debris floating in there. How could I
have been so unaware of all that clutter before now?*

*When I get back to Los Angeles, I'll sign up for a meditation
class—maybe at the yoga studio where I take classes. I've been
doing that for exercise for the past year, but maybe what I really
need is something to relax my head.*

I close my eyes softly, the warmth from my body encased in the
sleeping bag a soothing contrast to the crisp outside air. I should
sleep out here.

Without warning, a deep, guttural sound comes from the thicket
of trees next to me, less than three feet from where I'm sitting. I
jump. The sleeping bag and the journal slip together to the ground.
My gut moves into my throat.

I keep my head down. As I turn toward the direction of the
sound, I see the large shadow of a hulking, four-legged figure. It
growls again. The sound is beyond menacing.

I forget everything I've ever learned about contact with bears in
the wild. I run. I race, stumble, trip, crawl at a high speed, manage
to get on my feet, so I can move my body as fast as I can to the bath
house. Once inside, I shut the door and lock it. For the rest of the
night, I sit on the floor by the shower. Nothing else happens. I sit
there, eyes wide open, and shiver.

Chapter 2

Introducing Ishmel

THE NEXT NIGHT I MEET a Coyote. He's pesky and clever, and he invades my campsite for food. I awaken to the tinny clatter of him in my pots and pans. I don't know how he got into them. I distinctly remember securing them in my outdoor pack earlier.

The banging is followed by shuffling, and then a loud rip. I grope for my glasses and a flashlight. Next I hear a clang as something heavy hits a rock. I rush outside to discover what looks like a large dog standing over my tipped cooler. He holds a packet of turkey meat in his mouth. This particular Coyote is gray with pointed ears and a salacious grin. He has a long bushy tail, a sharp square nose, and seems large, at least four feet long.

The full moon is huge, and it illuminates the extent of the damage the Coyote has done to my things. My cookware is scattered every which way around the site, and the rest of my food is spread even farther; ripped bits of wrappers and half-chewed pieces of fruit litter the area.

The Coyote drops the turkey and releases a triumphant howl at the moon. It is an ear-piercing, blood-curdling sound, like screaming with a rhythm, like an angry toddler with a bullhorn yelling, "Look at me. I am here," over and over again.

I have half a mind to chase him as he runs into the forest, but instead I clean up his mess.

• *July 15, 2008*

I'm sick of this Coyote. He's returned every night this week, interrupting the sound of the breathing. He always makes a mess, and he always waits until I exit the tent, swearing, stumbling, and angry, to let out a howl in my direction before running away. Each time's made me more and more angry, prompting me to venture farther and farther into the woods after him.

Last night, I followed him to a remote rock formation. The rocks there formed the shape of a large pyramid, and the Coyote sat on top. I am convinced he waited until I was close enough to look into his yellow eyes before he let out his final ear-splitting howl in my direction.

Then it happened. I realized the Coyote's eyes were not the only ones peering into mine. From the shadows of a patch of trees, I saw a pair of steely blue eyes looking straight at me. The new eyes were in front of their owner's head, those of a predator. The darkness blocked my vision, so I cannot say whether I was facing an animal or a human.

I bolted. As quickly as I could, tripping in my panic, I raced to my tent and dove inside, where I cowered.

• *July 16, 2008*

The weather shifted today, and I'm writing at a window seat inside the lodge. The air seemed ready for the change this morning, waiting. It was ninety degrees by ten o'clock, hotter than it's been, and the atmosphere was heavy, weighed down by humidity. When I sat by the lake, the sky, contrary to its usual empty sweep of blue, was dark; clouds swept through it in thicker and thicker layers. It grew darker and darker until a mist eased down on everything, refreshing after two weeks of intense summer heat.

Then, without warning, the mist thickened into full-fledged drops, falling relentlessly down at a high velocity. I had barely enough time to zip the rain cover over my tent, my body sweaty and soaked at the same time.

I didn't see the point in cowering alone out there as I had the night before. Not that I really think a Grizzly would be daft enough to hang around outside in the rain, and my dad does always say that animals won't bother humans unless we harass them.

But still, what was the thing doing so close to my tent the other night? Was it looking for food, like the Coyote was? I should probably move all the food here into the lodge once the rain stops. No one seems to be monitoring this place anyway.

The rain pelts against the window, blurring my view, and I put down the pen. As I look away from the storm, into the lodge itself, I link eyes with the elk head over the fireplace. I imagine it somehow attached to its body still, even as it hangs, disembodied over the mantle.

I should sleep in here all night, I tell myself as I doze off on that window seat. There's no reason to face the tent and the growls at this point.

I wake in the morning to blazing sunshine; it glares in my face through the window. Yesterday's storm seems an incongruent memory, no more substantial than a receding trace from one of my dreams.

I pace. I can't go out there again.

• July 17, 2008

When I got back to my tent this morning, I discovered that everything inside was soaking wet. Evidently there was a hole in the rain tarp.

I spent the early part of the day dragging my personal items and bedding into a nearby clearing where I could spread them out in the direct sunshine. It was so warm outside, they dried in a couple hours. Once I put my tent back in order, I took a shower followed by a sauna, followed by another shower in the bath house.

Every time I use the facilities in here, I feel like I am trespassing somehow. I know I bought a camping permit for the month, but it's not clear to me whether the bath house belongs to whoever runs the abandoned retreat house, or whether it goes with the campground. Either way it is always empty, leaving me with the uncanny feeling that I'm not supposed to be here because no one is supposed to be here.

As I eat tonight, the Coyote returns. This time he moves quite close, as if he were a pet dog. I toss him scraps of bacon I've mixed into my usual baked beans. He sniffs with disdain before devouring my offering. When he finishes, he licks his large chops and curls into a ball about five feet from me, close enough for us both to watch the other, but far enough for either one of us to make a quick getaway. Oddly, his presence comforts me.

I have yet to hear the strange breathing today, but I am apprehensive about sleeping undefended. I leave the Coyote there as a sentinel.

I awaken in the middle of the night to his moaning and yowling outside my tent. When I stick my head out, I see the Coyote circling round and round the campsite, completely disoriented.

I throw a shoe in his direction. "Scram!" I shout. Just then, the ground rumbles and the whole forest starts shaking. The Coyote bolts into the trees.

It is an earthquake, and a rather large one. It rattles my cookware outside and the entire contents of my tent, throwing me off balance. When the shaking finally stops, I have a hard time standing. My legs have become limp noodles. I had no idea there were earthquakes like that in Montana. Eventually, I pull myself upright.

I don't know why, but I leave the campsite and head for the woods. Maybe I'm searching for the Coyote to whom, despite myself, I feel attached. I do hear him howl again from not too far away. Maybe I am simply rattled by the earthquake, and now, my head pounding and my pulse racing, I find it impossible to rest. For whatever reason, I walk farther and farther from my campsite, using my flashlight to keep from stumbling, wondering if the breathing and the growl I heard before were my imagination. Finally, I reach the circular rock formation and stop. I attempt to steady my breathing.

It can't be more than a few seconds before he appears—a massive and temperamental Grizzly. He comes from behind the tall rocks at my back. I would not have even turned to notice, but for the sudden whoosh of the wind combined with a rustling noise in the leaves behind me. When I do turn, I realize the rustling is the smashing sound of foliage under his gigantic paws as he moves toward me.

I freeze under his fiery gaze. Even on all fours he is huge, so imagine my shock and consternation when he rises before me on his hind legs, his hooded silver mane fully bristled, the steel-blue eyes staring at me with a soul-grilling penetration.

This Bear is vitality incarnate in my eyes—violent, fertile; he can take anything or anyone in his immediate world, and he looks like he's considering me for lunch. My legs buckle beneath me. I feel my body tingle with a layer of sweat. It is then that I, a confirmed atheist, fold my hands in prayer.

"Dear God," I stutter mentally.

The Grizzly roars. It is like thunder. The roots of the trees around us rattle. I cower before the sound. I consider that what I thought was an earthquake may have only been his bellowing.

The Grizzly speaks. His words come to me in English, not out of his bear mouth, but directly into my mind: "Fear not, Darling One. My roar is the roar of nature—the roar of all understanding."

I open my mouth to speak, but cannot.

"Communicate, but use your mind," the Bear continues.

I don't believe in psychic communication. Even reading people's subtle expressions is difficult for me. I grew up in an Italian family where making faces accompanies loud talking. People must tell me directly what they want, a point of contention between Brian and I. He always faults me for disregarding his needs without ever stating what those needs are. I hate that he expects me to read his mind.

"Relax, open your mind," instructs the Bear. "Allow your thoughts to escape back into me. Let them soar toward the heavens in a stream of understanding. Be clear and open and true."

I adore him before knowing him. He is glorious, this Grizzly— as wide as the night sky—as if he stretches across the entire mass of stars above us and holds it all together like immortal glue.

My legs wobble as I stand to face him. I reach out my hand to touch his fur—soft and shiny. He roars again at that. This time the sound seems less threatening—more of a comfortable bellow, and now instead of cowering down before him, I stand, face him eye to eye, and feel a warm glow. It starts in my gut and spreads throughout my body until I tremble inside from the strength of it.

I feel him scanning my mind for a response, but I will myself to remain closed to him. Yet despite my efforts, an instant silence clamps onto my thoughts; all that constant prattle going on and on in my head ceases into one splendid, miraculous, quiet moment. It feels as if the Bear has somehow inserted himself in there, willfully made space.

Into that silence, the voice of the Bear continues. His voice in my mind is not so much a sound as a sensation, and despite the large, intimidating figure of the Bear before me, it is soft. The words come from a source *outside* me, and at the same time they resonate deep within my psyche. I feel shell-shocked, off-kilter, unsure as to whether his voice is real or imaginary.

"Let go of your skepticism. You must open your mind in order for us to commune. It is crucial that you learn."

Finally I manage to say, "I'm frightened," and in an energetic rush from my brain into his, I realize the Grizzly both hears and understands me.

"Of course you are. This encounter, if little else, is highly unusual."

"Why is this happening?" I stammer.

"You willed it so. You have summoned me just as you yourself are summoned."

"Summoned?"

"I will teach you seven precepts."

"What's a precept? You mean laws? Like the Ten Commandments?"

"Not so much commandments as realizations, stages in the development of perception. You will write these down."

"Please," I beg. "Find someone else. I'm completely wrong for this sort of thing."

"You are here, now. As I am."

"Who *are* you, anyway?"

"My name," he declares, "is Ishmel."

I've heard this name before somewhere; the Bear himself seems suddenly familiar. I feel supercharged, like everything I've learned until now has been a preparation for this one moment. I consider that I am either: (1) going crazy or (2) faced with a phenomenon

I cannot understand. If possibility 1 is true, as I strongly suspect, I don't like it. I know what happens to "crazies" in our society. They're locked up, taken away to a spa or sanatorium where they sit in a deluded state, listening to voices coming from walls—never mind grizzly bears.

I can hear my friends murmuring behind my back, "We always sort of thought she'd go off the deep end. All that nonsense about going off into the woods to find herself." My parents will be devastated, of course, as if my mother doesn't have enough to worry about with a sick husband. I'm supposed to be the bright one in the family, headed for great achievements. "She always was a bit too nervous," Mom will admit to the doctors as she signs my confinement papers. At least now the tremendous strain of having an unstable daughter can be resolved. My father will naturally donate a large sum of his living trust to the facility itself. My folks can only hope I'll be treated humanely by the staff there. Electric shock therapy is always a nasty business. But I digress.

Let's consider the second possibility: that the Grizzly is real, but beyond my understanding. I don't like phenomena I can't control. I like situations neat and simple with a clear set of steps for manipulating reality in appropriate ways. What do I want with an interaction with something beyond the cushy, comfortable laws of science? I enjoy my world like it is—solid and down to earth without a lot of namby-pamby, corny, metaphysical rot mixed in to confuse matters.

This talking bear with a name I remember from a Bible story I can't quite recall definitely has great stirring-up potential. If he's real, he probably expects something of me; just what I need at this point in my muddled life—more pressure to perform. Excellent— just excellent. I back away from the Bear slowly and deliberately. Once I am far enough away, I run. I cower inside my tent for hours until, thoroughly spent, I fall into a fitful sleep.

Chapter 3

The Woman in the Cave

THE NEXT MORNING, WITH SUNLIGHT streaming into my tent, I lie. I remind myself that I'm a card-carrying atheist and proud of it. I don't believe in the Catholic God of my childhood. I don't believe in Moses or Mohammed or Buddha or Zeus and his gang either. I'm with Marx on the idea of organized religion: it's an opiate of the masses, around to motivate poor people, and probably the impetus for war. I certainly have no intention of reverting to primitive Native American bear worship.

I tell myself I must have been delusional. I'm an imaginative sort. I've dreamed the talking bear with his summons from above because the strange forest earthquake rattled me.

I pack my things. My debate is whether or not I will tell Brian what happened. It might be fun to laugh off the whole mental incident over a martini and spicy tuna rolls. I will definitely not be telling my father; I can't take the condescension and razzing he'd inevitably dish out if he knew about my imagined conversation with a sacred bear.

By three o'clock, I have everything in a pile by the rental car. I prepare to return to Los Angeles. "You've had your little foray into solitude," I tell myself. I pretend nothing unusual is happening as I stack my camping belongings—blankets, cookware, rain tarp, and clothing—into the trunk of the car. I slam it shut and slide into the driver's seat.

By now, it is four o'clock and sunny. People don't sight grizzlies or other forest animals this time of day. I know that. I stop lying to myself and admit that I am deliberately making an escape. I need to leave now or risk a confrontation with the Grizzly. I'm getting out while the getting's good. I plan to forget my meeting with the Bear or, if that is impossible—and I find myself remembering the events in the woods—I will let them become vague, like a dream.

I drive down the gravelly road toward Helena, away from the site. As I get farther and farther away from those woods, I breathe more easily and fumble for my cell phone to call Brian. That is when I notice something move in the pine trees at the side of the road—something massive and silver gray.

I drop the phone in my lap but keep driving. "No," I tell myself. "It's probably just the Doe or the Coyote or something else."

But I know it is neither the Doe nor the Coyote. It is Ishmel, and he is trying to stop my exit. I see the glint of steely blue eyes from those trees. I stifle my fear as I press a bit harder on the gas pedal.

That is when he steps in front of my car. He is undeniable then; he takes up most of the road. I slam on the brakes and skid with a screech to stop before him.

We stare at each other in silence, the Bear and I, through the windshield. He doesn't move, doesn't roar, doesn't say a word, just stares at me through the glass, and I, stunned, stare back. Then, he swipes his giant paw in front of my face, leaving a six-inch scratch down the glass on the driver's side. He shoots another significant glance in my direction before rambling off into the trees.

Slowly, carefully, I put the car in reverse. I head backwards down the gravel road, back toward my encampment. So I suppose he's real, Ishmel; there *was* a bear on my windshield just now.

I want to deny it. It would be easier in lots of respects to deny anyone was there at all. But there's the issue of the scratch mark. There's the issue of those blue eyes looking right into me. If Ishmel is just some random bear with no meta-cognition, what is he doing looking me in the eye that way, like he knows my mind?

I sense the Bear thinking of me even now, his thoughts hooked into my own. *I really want to hear his voice again.*

Even if I wanted to get away, go back to how I was before, that would be impossible. He's already become part of me somehow. Shit, it feels like he's been there all along.

I really, really want to see him. I've had a clear hit of something so pure, so true; there's simply no going back. One hit, and—even as I'm denying its veracity—I'm hooked.

Besides, I don't need to be back in Los Angeles until mid-September. It doesn't make sense for me to go back to the city now.

I unload my things, set up camp, and turn on the stove to heat baked beans for dinner. Later, the Coyote comes for his bacon scraps. He eats and curls up in a ball near my tent. I sit there and watch the first stars in that wide Montana sky. I become quiet. More stars become visible until I am covered in a blanket of starlight from above. I sit there and wait. I wait and wait, until, shivering, I crawl back into the tent for warmth.

• *July 20, 2008*

There was no sign of the Grizzly the past three nights. I am desperate for contact. I feel isolated out here and lonely.

I'm such a loser. The whole idea of a summons from the Grizzly is probably just an ego move on my part.

I've dissected everything that happened over and over again. Ishmel wanted to teach me—I don't know—something expansive, interesting, and loser that I am, I argued about it, rejected it, pretended he didn't exist.

What if Ishmel never comes back? Maybe since I've packed, tried to get away from him, he's changed his mind and found someone else. He should. Leave it to me to muck up my first, my only chance at salvation. That's my problem—I run away from everything when it starts to feel legitimate. I've run away from Brian, my parents, and now I've run away from—I don't know who Ishmel is—someone important, probably. He's gone now. Just like everything else, I've blown it.

He probably doesn't exist anyway. Jerry said there were bears out here, and yes, a bear did attack my car. There's the undeniable matter of the scratch on my windshield. That was real enough. I've felt it several times today with my hand. The glass has a definite indentation on it. But that doesn't prove the Bear was a mind-reading guide with the ability to transmit life lessons to my lost soul. How lame is that? If there even is a God or a Blackfoot Great Spirit or a King of the Forest or anybody, why would he be interested in my personal life? Chances are, he wouldn't care about me at all.

When I wake the next morning, it is overcast, gloomy, and I am dying for a decent cup of coffee. It can't be healthy to spend this much time alone in the woods. I head into town to Jerry's store, where I have distinct memories of a pot of freshly brewed coffee on the front counter. I need to know if grizzly bears even have blue eyes. And if Ishmel does exist, there should be more proof—an abandoned den somewhere, footprints, something. Otherwise I really might be cracking up.

Jerry pours me a cup of hot coffee and watches me from across the counter as I slurp it down with a warm raspberry muffin that tastes wonderfully homemade.

"When was the last time you had anything to eat?" Jerry is concerned, but calm.

"Um . . . yesterday. Do I look crazy to you?"

Jerry surveys my disheveled hair, the off-center glasses on my nose, and the patches of dirt on my shirt and jeans.

"I don't know."

"You don't *know?*" I am shouting now.

"I wouldn't call you crazy. You just seem wound up about something."

"Tell me about grizzly bears."

"Well," he pulls out a pamphlet, "it's not size per se that identifies them, although they are large. It's the hood." He points to the bristling hair around the bear's neck in the picture. "A grizzly hood works the same as a hood on a cobra does. It intimidates. It reminds the victim of the bear's ultimate power."

"I think I saw one. It had a silver-gray hood like in the picture, and blue eyes." I finish my muffin and reach for a second when Jerry pushes the tray toward me. "Is that even possible?"

"Grizzlies around here are rare, but it is possible."

"It had blue eyes. Does a grizzly with steely blue eyes actually exist?"

Jerry clears his throat. "There have been other reports of a bear meeting that description, yes."

"Where? Does he have, I don't know, a den or something somewhere?"

"The dens are abandoned this time of year, it being mating season and all," he pauses. "We have pinpointed one specific spot where that particular bear has his cave: Boulder Falls. There's no water there this time of year. It's right over where you're camping, actually." He clears his throat. "You can reach it by driving up the back side of Mother Mountain."

"Mother Mountain?"

"That's what the locals call it. You've probably seen the peak from the lake."

I take my last hundred dollars from my wallet and slide it toward him across the counter. "I want you to take me there."

Jerry pushes my money back at me. "I'll take you to the hibernation spot. But you can keep your money."

We are silent in the truck ride back to the forest. I feel a little more stable now that I've had caffeine, but I am still aware that my heart beats quicker the closer we get to the mountain. I recognize the snow-topped peak above us as the one I've observed from my writing spot by the lake. It is rocky and barren at the base where Jerry parks the truck.

There is a slope, about thirty degrees, at the side of the mountain. It leads to a small opening, half the size of an average doorframe. The opening is made even smaller by a large rock jutting halfway over it from the side of the mountain's face. Jerry directs me to crawl into the small, primitive enclosure. The den is too small for both of us to fit inside, so I enter alone.

I get a prickly feeling down my spine when I cross into that space, as though someone were watching me there—as though on some level he knows I've entered his private domain. Diffused sunlight from the entrance allows me to see the sides of the enclosure; it is layered with twigs and grass, a comfortable lair for the winter. That is when I see a tuft of silver-gray hair in the corner of the den. *This is where he sleeps.*

I imagine that in the winter it is still—secure and warm inside. I shiver and climb back outside into the open air and Jerry.

"Well?" Jerry asks.

"It looks like . . ." I hesitate. "It could be real."

"Oh, yes, no doubt."

"Have you ever seen him?"

"No, but I keep hoping. Someday," Jerry mutters as he fishes through his pocket for his keys. "One of these days, I'll make contact."

• *July 21, 2008, midnight*

Tonight, miraculously, the Grizzly appeared. There was a rustle of leaves as before, followed by the Coyote's howl. I sat up to find I'd fallen asleep on the ground outside the tent. From the trees next to me, I could see the familiar glint of blue eyes, then Ishmel in his entire silver-gray glory. He moved beside me slowly as if to soothe me, and to prevent me from bolting again.

I had no intention of running this time; I was ecstatic to see him. I am getting a bit used to his large size and the powerful energy pull that surrounds him. It's like a magnet, this pull.

The closer he got, the more I felt myself drawn to his side. I sensed that he knew what he was doing, and I felt again the strong rush of energy shooting from him into my being.

Wow, I thought in amazement. he likes me. We sat still for a long moment until I broke the stillness by squirming.

He started talking. "So, you saw my sleeping space."

My voice stuck in my throat. I was grateful to communicate telepathically. "Yes," I answered.

"I like that you were there."

We sat wordlessly for what seemed like hours. When he finally did depart, and I crawled into my tent to sleep, I slept more soundly than I have in years.

I drag around in the morning, shell-shocked, excited. I still complete my usual routine, making breakfast, feeding the Coyote, bathing, hiking the trails around my campsite, but now these tasks have become secondary. I can barely wait for nightfall again and a possible visitation from Ishmel. Sure enough, when the sky goes completely dark and the stars appear, so does the Bear.

He sits across from me this time, more purposeful than before.

"This material's important. You should get your notebook, write it down." He directs.

"Right." I adjust my glasses on my nose before heading into my tent for my spiral journal. I catch a glimpse of myself in a compact mirror and realize I am a mess—hair disheveled, face riddled with mosquito bites. "Oh well," I mumble to myself. "It probably doesn't matter to him. He's a *Grizzly* Bear."

I exit the tent with my journal, a pen, and a flashlight, although the stars are so bright I don't really need it.

"Excellent," he murmurs into my head. "Now, make yourself comfortable and write."

I lean back against the log, balance the journal on my lap, and prepare to write volumes.

"Are you ready?"

I gulp. "Yes, I'm ready."

"All your needs . . ." He pauses. "Are you writing this down?"

"Yes," I stammer as I write.

"All your needs will be met."

There is a long pause.

"Okay," I say. "You can keep going."

"That's it. Precept One is *All your needs will be met.*" He rolls an apple out from the plastic sack of food I forgot to hang in the tree. He noses it and takes a large bite. I recoil as I glimpse his teeth—long, pointy, and numerous.

I expected lengthy and complex, not one-liners. I reread the words while he chomps on the apple.

"That's ridiculous," I mutter.

"What's ridiculous?"

"All your needs will be met. Tell that to a starving kid in Africa, and see how much sense it makes."

He bares his teeth again, and for a second I feel nervous. Finally he speaks. "The starving kids in Africa aren't the ones who doubt the precept. Their situation is the direct result of the beliefs of others, those who wallow in a poverty mentality when they have everything."

"What 'others'?" I squirm uncomfortably.

"You know. Those With Wealth who grab for more and more because they doubt the precept. They accumulate such an excess, it burdens them. If they would simply absorb the precept and accept that all their needs will be met, there wouldn't be any children starving in Africa or anywhere.

"Come, climb on my back," he commands, and I obey.

I feel insecure, wobbly, and tremendously excited all at once. His back is firm, rippled with muscles under the thick fur. His hood is softer than I would have expected, and when I lean in close, it smells clean, a mixture of pine and wild sage.

I inhale deeply, and an image of a man flashes in my mind. He is tall and muscular, naked except for a loin cloth. His hair is black and falls well past his shoulders. The eyes are changeable—at first I am sure they are a steely blue shade, but in the next instant they appear green, the color of the forest around us. I can't quite pinpoint the man's age. The black hair does betray some experience with several streaks of silver gray. My body tenses.

"You must relax," Ishmel's voice echoes in my head.

I draw my breath in and out, and as I do I feel my skin, my muscles, all of me, tingle.

"Stay aware now," the Bear instructs.

I close my eyes and see a bonfire in these same woods, right where my tent sits, but it is another time and my tent is not there. Lots of people stand around the fire, and the mysterious man is in the center. The onlookers want to get closer to the warmth of the flames, closer to him. The man wears Ishmel's coat of fur—the entire length of the Bear's skin is draped over the man's body, the silver-gray of Ishmel's hood covers his head.

The man sways; he dances in gyrating movements as the people chant words I don't understand. Beads of sweat form on the man's naked chest. He leans his head back, arms spread like goalposts, bends his knees, and with a deep, musical voice sings an incantation to the stars. I know him. This is who Ishmel would be if he were a man.

With that, I open my eyes and grasp the Bear's fur. The muscles on his back flex below me, and I feel him begin to run. He picks up speed, going faster and faster until the shadowy objects of the forest blur together like the deliberately obscure texture of an Impressionist painting.

He carries me with exhilarating speed. The wind whips at my face, and when I look up, I see a breathtaking display of stars above us.

When he stops, we are at the foot of a snow-capped mountain, just beside a small house built from logs into the side of the mountain wall. I recognize the peak from before as Mother Mountain and realize that Ishmel's den is just on the other side of it. By and by, a woman appears.

Her face is wrinkled with past burdens, and her upper back hunches. Her hair curls around her chin in a youthful style, an ironic contrast to her leathery face. I am uncertain how old this woman is; it is unclear from her demeanor, so weighed down and hunched is she. I'm guessing she's built her house into the mountain cave as protection from the elements.

We watch as she carries wood from a pile behind the house to her fireplace; under the weight of the wood she becomes more hunched than ever, but adamantly refuses my offer to assist her.

She invites me inside for tea and cake, and I accept, leaving Ishmel to wait outside the cave. Her house is so cluttered inside that I can barely squeeze in behind her. A large armoire holds shelf upon shelf of teacups, all covered with dust. Boxes of photographs, paid bills, advertisements, old magazines, and yellowing letters are strewn about the narrow living area, making it impossible to walk in a straight line. She leads me to a dusty couch by the fireplace.

Seven jewel boxes line the wall on a bureau cabinet opposite the fireplace, each one stuffed to the brim with pearls, diamonds, and other gems. A jewel-encrusted tiara sits atop the center box. An emerald necklace hangs from the box next to that one.

The bureau drawers below are jammed to the brim with clothing: shirts and pants with designer labels—Donna Karan, Saint John, Yves Saint Laurent, and the like. Oddly enough, despite all this finery, the woman wears jeans and a work shirt. She glances at the overflowing boxes.

"These were gifts," she tells me, "from my children and their children."

"Oh," I answer, wondering why Ishmel has instructed me to interact with this woman.

"I never hear from them," she bemoans. "Of course, they're all so busy, with their jobs and families and that." As she makes this statement, she touches the emerald necklace, ever so gently. "If it weren't for Ishmel out there, I'd be all alone. I do wish I could invite him in, but," she motions with her hand, "he simply won't *fit* with all my things."

I gulp. "I guess not."

"Would you like some tea, dear?"

When I nod, she rises to enter the smallest kitchen I have ever seen, made smaller by the stacks of patterned china plates on the counters. They have a lovely pattern, pink rosebuds dotted with blue violets, but it is impossible to see them clearly because they are stacked every which way, covered with papers and silverware.

When the woman opens the refrigerator door, a horrible stench enters the room. I see that it is packed to the brim with rotting food: breads, unopened packages of lunch meat, fruits, lettuces, and jellies with layers of mold on top.

"Oh dear," she mutters. "I'm not sure where I stuck the cake. This is so embarrassing."

She rifles through the refrigerator before pulling out a lemon Bundt cake and the remains of a jar of raspberry jam. She refuses my repeated offers to help her with boiling the tea water, a pointless exercise in the end because all of her boxes of tea are empty. So she sits and watches as I choke down the stale cake and jam, informing me she can have none of it herself due to a recent diagnosis of type 2 diabetes.

I eat as much as I can stand and listen to her warning about Ishmel. "He's powerful," she informs me. "Be very careful."

She looks annoyed when I ask why, and only says, "A young, pretty girl like you, you should be with your family, not out here alone, studying with some bear."

I am glad when Ishmel roars for me to come back outside; I leave the woman sitting alone in her cave, surrounded by all the things she doesn't need. Ishmel carries me back to my tent, and it seems refreshingly barren after my visit.

Chapter 4

All Your Needs Will Be Met

• *July 23, 2008*

My obsession with Ishmel grows. Who is he? He has a sense of playfulness when I am in his presence. More and more, I visualize him in my mind's eye not as a bear, but as the man from the bonfire.

I want him to be real—this man who is a bear. I want to touch his hair. I want to be aware of him aware of me again, as I was when he carried me on his back. In my fantasy, I reveal everything to him, peel off layer after layer of myself, my demeanor, all these masks I've been wearing, until all that's left of me is what's real. I want him to see me, and at the same time, I want to see him. I want him to know me.

I dream of the man for three nights, even though I don't make physical contact with the Bear. In my dreams I catch glimpses of him in Blackfoot attire, watching me tentatively from behind trees. Later, I walk to him where he sits on the circular rock formation. We make eye contact, then take hands and walk together. It feels lovely and exclusive, but at the same time, I have this sense that everyone in the forest—other humans not yet perceived or animals—are watching our growing relationship. What seems private is actually quite public, and I've become used to interacting with him while constantly under this invisible scrutiny.

Ishmel the Bear finally appears again, and for the next few days, we argue about Precept One. I list all my supposed needs living in Los Angeles, and Ishmel guides me in realizing that they are fabrications. I've gotten into the habit of replacing my car every few years, I tell him. I hate to admit it to Ishmel, but I am also quite the shopaholic. I know brands and styles; I am forever searching for the perfect outfit to wear to the perfect occasion. Fine dining is also a weakness. I "need" Brian to take me to a top Los Angeles restaurant at least once a week.

I myself earn a paltry teacher's salary, but that is all part of my image: self-sacrificing, a public servant who deserves fine clothes and dining. Yet I do feel much happier in the forest with a can of beans and three pairs of old jeans. It occurs to me that what I perceive as *needs* are really *wants*. Maybe I don't know what's good for me. When Ishmel makes this suggestion, I balk. Of course I know what's good for me. Otherwise, where do I turn for guidance? Who does know?

• *August 1, 2008*

Five days and no Ishmel. I feel strung out when he's not around. I've been sulking all morning like a spoiled child. I should be more independent of him. He's obviously ignoring me. Why? And why should I care? Who is he to me?

This whole trip is a betrayal of Brian on lots of levels. If I were really in love with Brian, if I really wanted to spend my life with him, what am I doing sitting out here in the woods waiting around for some bear? Brian and I have dated three years now, yet it is Ishmel who knows my mind.

He's gotten to me, damn it! All morning I've been walking the trails in the forest listening for him: his footsteps, his voice, his teaching. Shouldn't it be Brian I want? My yearning for the Bear must be wrong.

It's too warm today to write. I'm sweaty and uncomfortable. I put down the journal and peruse my surroundings. There's never anybody here. I peel off my clothes and walk to the edge of the lake. It's marvelous to be out here, butt naked in the middle of the day. So what about Ishmel? Screw him.

With a whoop, I plunge feet-first into the mountain lake. The cold water stings at first and then feels wonderfully refreshing. I paddle to the center of the lake, catching sight of a family of turtles sunning themselves on the rocks near the bank. I roll onto my back, float aimlessly, and focus on the stunning blue Montana sky.

It takes about ten minutes for me to realize that several leeches have latched onto the backs of my legs. I panic, thrashing all over the place, only to discover with revulsion that two more have attached to the inside of my elbows. The more I try to brush them off, the firmer they take hold of my skin.

I swim wildly, splashing water everywhere as I make my way back to shore. In the end, the only way for me to remove them is to stick my fingernails beneath the front of their bodies where they suck at me and break the seal. I peel them off one by one, and each time the skin underneath bleeds.

I am shaking too hard to bother with my clothes at this point. I run naked through the woods, oblivious to the twigs and small rocks piercing my feet.

When I reach my tent, Ishmel is waiting there. We look each other up and down in mutual shock. I've never seen him in the day before. Is it my imagination or do his eyes seem heavy, tired?

"What happened to you?" he finally asks.

"Me? I'm not the one who stayed away for *five* days. I waited up half the night for you, and you never showed." I dive into my tent, rustle around for clean clothes, and reemerge in one of Brian's oversized UCLA shirts.

Ishmel approaches me slowly. "Come here," he says softly.

I take a step toward him, defying him all the while with my eyes. How dare he?

"You should disinfect the wounds," he suggests. "Maybe use alcohol or hydrogen peroxide." With that he nuzzles the inside of my right elbow with his nose. Before I can think to protest, he licks me there. His tongue feels pleasantly grainy; it's like being cleaned by a cat. My arm pulses, warm, where his tongue touches, and a tingly feeling spreads down to my fingers, then back up into my shoulder. I pull away, angry.

"I didn't think to visit you last night, Darling One. It didn't occur to me at the time."

I plop down on the log by the tent, frustrated. I look at the inside of my arm; the redness and bleeding are entirely gone. "You should have known," I protest. "You can't expect *me* to have known what was happening. Anyway, I think I've proved my point. All my needs are *not* always met. Otherwise, you would have been there."

He pauses and suggests something I find utterly unnerving. "You have to allow the process, Darling One, and that requires an element of surrender."

"I don't do surrender, Ishmel," I snap back at him. "It runs against my training."

"What training?"

"As an independent, self-sufficient individual. That's how my parents raised me. That's how I want to be."

Ishmel's eyes focus on the ground. "Did your parents also raise you to yap and flit about with no control, like an overcharged lap dog? Consider shutting up, Darling One."

I feel my face flush. Without thinking, I pick up the empty pot where it sits from last night's meal and throw it at his head.

He cringes at the impact, and I stand motionless, horrified at my own impromptu violence.

"As you wish." His voice is soft as he turns his back to me and retreats.

I rush toward him. It's taken five days for me to make contact. Who knows how long it might be if I let Ishmel leave now? "Do we have to use the word *surrender?* Can't it be *cooperate?*"

The Bear continues backing away.

"Ishmel," my voice is loud now, pleading. "I'm a separate entity. What about the word *accept?* I accept you, and you accept me. At least then I keep my individuality."

"No, Darling One, you will always be an individual. But you must recognize the underlying integration of all things, and so ultimately you must surrender."

"What? You want to brainwash me? Is this some sort of bear cult?"

Ishmel is silent.

"Okay, I'm sorry. I didn't mean to accuse you of anything weird. This whole . . . whatever this is . . . it's weird already. Fine, I'll try it once. For, say, the next five minutes, I'll try and—"

"Silence your mind."

"Yeah, silence my mind then, and surrender to . . . I don't even know what I'm surrendering to."

"To what's happening, Darling One."

"And what *is* that, anyway?"

"Five minutes is an excellent start." He rambles back in my direction, and we both sigh. I sit on the log, and he sits on the ground beside me. "You'll have to keep doing it," he continues. "Again and again you're going to have to let go, until you reach a state of complete acknowledgment."

"I can do acknowledgment—just don't use the word *surrender* again."

"But you see, Darling One, only once you have fully surrendered to reality as it is, will you be able to fully acknowledge it."

"I don't want to be a robot, or a slave," I argue.

"That's the point, Darling One. The point where you acknowledge What Is will be the point where you are truly free."

"Five minutes," I relent.

"Let's try it together," he suggests, and we sit in silence for what feels much longer.

• *August 2, 2008*

Ishmel talked last night about hoarding. He said the concept of abundance involves the realization that everything—love, friendship, beauty, space—is by definition unlimited. The tightening feeling that leads to hoarding is always rooted in an inaccurate perception of what is happening.

I argued that sometimes it's a matter of survival. We have to grab what we can for our immediate family before it runs out. He told me to expand my definition of family.

Now, as I sit here writing by the lake, I realize I've been hoarding from family members all along. I've withheld love from my mother and father, and certainly Brian. I've acted like there's only so much of it for me to give, and I've been jealous, always expecting them to cough up something in return. Where did I get the idea that love was a scarce resource?

I've hoarded my own talents, what I might accomplish because I've felt that I wasn't good enough, that I was restricted somehow. I've begrudged Brian his success because I've always thought success was limited; there are winners and losers, and if he

*makes it, then it must be impossible for me to succeed too. If I'm
a failure, why would he even want me?*

*I just realized I'm holding my breath. What's wrong with me? Do
I think there's not enough air to go around either?*

• *August 3, 2008*

*Everything in the forest seems different today. It's not that
anything's changed, per se—it's more like I can pick out this
subtle, multidimensional depth to all of it.*

*Until now, I hadn't realized how stuff pulsates—lots of it
tingles the same way my arm did when Ishmel licked my wound.
Every once and a while when I blink, I notice stuff glowing: the
trees, the Coyote, my tent, my own fingers and toes. How could I
have missed this before?*

*I'm suddenly aware of my breathing—the way it sounds as it
moves through my body, like Ishmel's breath when I wait for him.
I catch a rhythm in all I do; it's there as I wash pots and pans,
sweep out my tent, walk through trails. I feel softer, like I'm
moving deliberately slower, more sensitized than ever before.*

What if this newfound energy source is limited? My instinct is to
contain it, to harness it somehow, if only to prevent it from leaving
with no warning. It could disappear as quickly as it arrived. Then
I remember hoarding, and *All your needs will be met.* Obviously,
that's still tough to swallow. What finally convinces me is not Ishmel, but my encounter with another bear.

I shower that night, as always, in the bath house. I slather myself
with strawberry-scented lotion, then flip on my flashlight and begin
the half-mile trek back to my tent.

That is when I come face to face with a pair of yellow eyes. I know right away they belong to a bear, and unlike Ishmel, it doesn't speak English. Here I am, trapped. I wonder if all my needs will be met now. What happens next surprises me.

I stand alone, slathered in lotion, face to face with the glowering, predatory eyes of a black bear. I wait and discover that moment by moment, I am quite all right. I have my breath and my wits—both prove helpful in dealing with the bear.

My knees go weak. The bear sniffs the air in my direction. Miraculously, I remember everything Jerry told me a month ago about bears. Always be prepared with pepper spray. Unfortunately I've left that in my tent. Never get closer than fifty yards. Here I am, less than twelve *feet* from one. Don't look the bear in the eye, but don't turn and run either. I look down at the dirt. I back away.

At that, the bear lumbers toward me. I sink to the ground, rolling my body into a submissive ball. The bear paws me, as though testing to see what I will do. I take a breath and try not to panic. That is when I am aware of the tingling again in myself, and I notice that the bear over me is tingling too. The same stuff that's in me is in the bear!

Finally, it walks away, back into the forest. I lay still for a long time before venturing back to my tent on wobbly legs, and I say a prayer of thanksgiving to whatever God may be out there. It's the second time in the past month that I've prayed, the only two times in my adult life.

• *August 4, 2008*

I'm still struggling with the concept of needs. I currently lack the funds in my bank account to cover next month's rent. That's a pretty common problem, I guess. It's hard to buy into the concept of abundance when you're about to be evicted.

That night I ask Ishmel about the rent. He reminds me of my encounter with the black bear.

"Within each given moment, Darling One, you will find yourself with exactly what you need to survive that moment. The fear, the skepticism comes from the perceived possibility of lacking, *not in the moment,* but sometime in the future. The fear of facing the bear lies in the simple thought: what will happen next? Maybe now all my needs are met but later—that may be another story. Yet in the space of the present, the only moment that truly exists anyway, all your needs will always be met."

"Now, later, next year, next month. Sorry, Ishmel, but that just sounds like wordplay."

"This is more than a game of semantics, Darling One. It is the looming fear of scarcity, the worldwide mortgage hanging over all your heads that creates the scarcity at all. The *scare* that lies at the root of the word *scarcity* is fear; the anticipation of lacking *creates the lacking itself.* It catapults you from the present moment into some imagined future filled with scarcity *you yourselves create.*"

• *August 5, 2008*

In Los Angeles, I study with a renowned yoga master. He always lays his mat at the front of a large yoga room. He is a popular teacher, so his classes tend to fill to capacity. It's funny the way yogis in the class rush into the yoga room before class to lay out their mats, trying to claim the best vantage point of the master. At first, I refused to play this game of grabbing and claiming space, but when it quickly became apparent that my failure to participate would result in me being crammed by a door or pushed in the far back with no view of the teacher at all, I joined in, snatching my central spot along with everyone else. So I guess even a group of well-meaning yogis can create scarcity. I am still ashamed of my participation in that situation.

Now that I think about it, I've had plenty of lessons on the Law of Abundance. I remember stories about the gasoline shortages in the United States in the 1970s. My parents lived in Oregon at the time, and normally my mother would fill their station wagon at this easily accessible corner station. They say that literally overnight, there were long queues to get gasoline as everyone, anticipating rising prices, scrambled for it. My father had to leave well before dawn to sit for up to two hours to fill their tank.

I remember another story, about loaves and fishes. How could a multitude of hungry people be satisfied with a miserly amount of food? I'm getting now that it wasn't the amount that mattered, but people's perception of that amount. Once the people accepted that they would be miraculously fed by a small amount, they were indeed miraculously fed.

Yet I still stumble around. I'm afraid of economic scarcity but also scarcity of love. I didn't know it until just now, but I've worried there isn't enough love to go around, that my parents, everyone, will abandon me in the end.

I've been so ashamed, so sure that I don't deserve love. It's a precious commodity, so I've always thought it must be earned and then hoarded.

It's ironic, really—adults who attempt to earn and then hoard love are the ones who find themselves alone and abandoned. They feed into their own perception that love is limited, that there is not enough of it to go around, and they begin to clutch possessively to any shreds of love remaining in their lives. But anyone who has felt the intense energy of a large family, or a group meditating or praying together, knows that love does not shrink away with the increasing number of participants, but grows. As more people dive into a feeling of love together, as more people open and expand their systems energetically to the feeling tone of love, love itself expands along with each individual who buys into its expansion. The story of the fish and loaves resonates because the multitudes were not fed with a few loaves of bread and one or two fish alone; they were fed figuratively and literally with abundant love. It was love that changed the wave of perception until a miracle happened and everyone there was satisfied.

So Ishmel's right about the starving children. Worldwide abundance is a pipe dream because the majority of the population buys into the illusion of scarcity fed by their own misperception of the world situation. Just like the yogis scrambling for the best spot before the yoga master, we've hoarded our resources, not understanding that were we to simply tap in to the mental state that fuels the Law of Abundance, our food supply would not shrink but multiply. We choose to deplete our resources with a dinosaur-like mentality that refuses to expand and conserve, even though the state of current science provides us with the solutions to world hunger and environmental decay. It feels easier to continue living in a tunnel, mole-like, pummeling the soil before us, not wanting to look around at others, than to feel the intense expansion that the Law of Abundance promises.

Chapter 5

The Space-Time Continuum

• *August 6, 2008*

Okay, Diary, I guess I've moved unwittingly from facts to feelings here. I wanted to be scientific. I was raised to be scientific. So why do my feelings always get in the way and screw things up?

Strange, but I keep thinking about Dad. When I was a little girl, he always took me to the Griffith Park Observatory on Sundays. We'd look at the Zeiss telescope with its amazing twelve-inch refractor. One special occasion we drove from there up the winding road to Mt. Wilson to see the Hubble telescope, the one that inspired Griffith to build the observatory in Los Angeles in the first place.

Back at Griffith Park, I loved to watch the shows in the planetarium. My favorite was "Pluto Express." As I watched I'd imagine myself on my own trip through the galaxy, passing all the planets to reach Pluto, sitting all alone on the outskirts of known space.

The show started with a shot of the Los Angeles skyline on a rounded horizon at dusk. Slowly, the sky darkened until all the stars, heretofore hidden, became blazingly apparent. The narrator explained that the stars are always there, invisible to the human

*eye during the bright hustle and bustle of waking life. I loved
that concept, and I remember reaching for my father's hand
in excited anticipation as the previously unseen stars began to
twinkle around us. I'd take him with me on my mental voyage
through the Milky Way. We'd stop at each planet and watch as it
rotated on its axis and revolved around the sun. Saturn was my
favorite because of its rings, but the moons of Jupiter were pretty
exciting also. Earth seemed tiny in light of the vastness of space
around it. The concept of the earth as limited and life-giving at
the same time always felt good.*

*The planetarium show was our church, and astronomy our
religion. As I grew older, Dad and I watched Carl Sagan on PBS.
He'd explain how each of the billions of stars out there was a
potential planet, that the Milky Way was only one of an infinite
number of galaxies, and that time in the traditional sense was
nonexistent. If you were shot out into space at the speed of light
for eighty earth years, when you returned, everyone here will have
aged, but not you. You, the space traveler, would remain exactly
the same age that you were when you left.*

*Earth years only have significance when you are stuck on earth.
People are bound by gravity as the earth rotates around and
around the singular point of itself, and revolves around the sun
just as the moon revolves around it. I always wondered whether
the Milky Way revolved around something bigger than itself
also, whether it and all the other galaxies patterned themselves in
revolutions around some mysterious centrifugal force.*

*In college, I studied string theory, mostly as a point of discussion
with my father.* The Elegant Universe *became our mutual Bible,
the scientific key to realizing that we are stuck in our current
three-dimensional world only by virtue of our lack of awareness,
that mankind is at the verge of tapping in to the grandness of
all infinity. My father adored this book by virtue of the fact*

that it is scientific and reputable. I loved it for its philosophical
implications. But whatever our reasons, the book became a point
of commonality for my father and me. Later when I failed him
by taking a teaching job he considered below me, it was our
mutual interest in astronomy that kept us from splintering apart.

In the morning, the Raven wakes me. She circles the campsite with her loud *whoo hoo,* heralding the new dawn. I trudge, bleary-eyed, to the bath house and then to the empty kitchen where I now store my food. The run-in with the black bear is enough to convince me I don't want any food by my campsite. Besides, the large kitchen refrigerator holds enough for me to make fewer trips into town for supplies.

Then I take my usual walk through the woods. I run into Jerry. He is out with rangers from the Forest Service. They clean the underbrush from the trail and carry away fallen logs. He waves hello and asks how I am. It feels good to know someone outside these woods thinks of me, besides Brian.

Crazy, but I can feel Ishmel thinking of me right now. Is this possible? Maybe he sends his thoughts out into the atmosphere like an email. If I think back to string theory, it does seem possible for an object to be in more than one place in a given time. Is this the case with Ishmel? Does he sit with me and simultaneously tend to other situations elsewhere?

I prepare supper, baked beans with bacon again. Now that I've braved the storage room in the kitchen, I can supplement the meal with fresh vegetables and salads. When the Coyote joins me, I toss him scraps. It's warm tonight, stifling in the tent. I drag my sleeping bag outside by the Coyote and drift off to sleep there.

When it is entirely dark, when all the glittering constellations become visible in the night sky, Ishmel pays me a visit. I wake instinctively at his presence. The glowing blue eyes meet mine, and he tells me the second lesson concerns death and time.

I tell him I have to leave the forest in a week or two to prepare for my teaching job back in Los Angeles. Once the school year starts, I will be uncontrollably busy.

"It's one thing to work on this now, here, with hours to contemplate all of it," I tell him. "In my regular life, I'm on constant overload. I never have enough time."

"I see." His reply is soft and guttural.

"First there's my job. That takes all day. Then I have to exercise, cook for myself, keep up with friends. I'm on the phone most of the time when I'm not at work."

"It puts a strain on you. This lack of time."

"Oh, yeah. I hate it. It makes me irritable. I snap at people. I feel like I'm being interrupted whenever I do anything. It's like a constant rush. Even during fun things, I feel hassled or hungry or hurried. I wish I could do what you want and write down all your precepts, but it's impossible in real life. I don't have time."

"Everyone has the same time."

"Not me," I argue. I can feel my insides shrink in protest. It has to be true. I am limited. I can't even accomplish what's required to get through basic life in Los Angeles. The only way to find the time to write would be to give up exercise, and then I'll get fat. No one likes a fat writer. I can see it now—me slumped over a computer, hunched up and out of shape as I spend hours, my only hours, my last hours, typing a manuscript no one will ever read.

"No!" I scream mercilessly to the Grizzly. "Not me."

"Darling One," the Bear's voice is adamant. "You will have enough time. Because time itself is not real."

I feel wowed and irritated at the same time.

"Cute," I murmur back at him. "So how do you explain the ticking hands of the clock, the setting sun, appointments that you actually can be late for, and the calendar that ticks off days? In fact, I found my first gray hair just yesterday. That's not an illusion, damn it. Trust me. It wasn't there before."

He motions for me to climb onto his back. "Come," he commands.

Chapter 6

Raven Soars Above Time

AS I CLIMB ABOARD, I hear the loud *whoo hoo* of the Raven. I realize Ishmel and I must have talked away most of the night and it is already morning. As Ishmel begins to run, I realize the Raven's spine-tingling announcement is only a prelude for our takeoff. I'm not quite sure how he lifts into the sky; I only know that one moment I am snuggling my face into that great gray hood, admiring his land speed through an open field, and the next we are rising into the sky and leaving the confines of earth altogether. He takes off into the clouds until we fly right next to the Raven herself. We cut together through the moistness of the morning fog.

I feel my body chill as we pass through the milky strata. For the first several minutes, I see nothing. I am refreshed by the wet air on my nose and cheeks; it's like splashing into a cool lake after a dusty hike. Any sluggishness in my brain is washed away, and I awake in a way I never expected. Everything I see afterward is much clearer than before.

The Raven keeps issuing her loud *whoo hoo* sound next to me, and without warning even from myself, I tilt my own head back and yell a very similar sound of exaltation just as we burst through the last cloud bank into the open air.

The sun hits my face with welcome warmth, and I realize we are quite high, almost at the top of the twin pairs of mountains. It is barren up there, graced with patches of snow. We swoop right between the peaks over the tree line. The trees near the top are dotted with snow. Farther down, we hit a rushing river and hover in the wind directly over it. It brings a fresh, clean smell. I make out the shape of salmon swimming with the current below us with focused purpose. In an instant, Ishmel dives down into the rushing water, and we move with them for a bit, until he shoots back up into the sky.

We climb now, higher than before, up a sunbeam, until we break out of the earth's atmosphere altogether. I catch a glimpse of earth below us, blue and glorious with life, before we head into the depths of space, up so high the Milky Way looks like a slip of light you could slide down, hands in the air, shouting the same *whoo hoo* if you had the nerve. Instead, we soar up farther until even the Milky Way is just a pinprick of light.

My whole body tingles now, and when I look at my arms, wrapped into the fur of Ishmel's hood, I realize they too have become sparkly conduits for light. The light from my body bounces off the vastness that is the space around us, a reflection of the external light show and vice versa. I'm not sure if the light beams around me are reflecting onto my body or if my body is reflecting outward onto the canvas of space. It's like being in a hall of mirrors with no certainty as to the origin of anything.

Ishmel turns into the vast open space again and again. With each turn, I am awestruck by the intricacy, the dazzling arrangement of stars and planets. I've never seen these constellations in the planetarium. This must be it; we've just reached the end of the universe. But Ishmel turns yet again, and I see it all from yet another angle, even more sublime, more stunning than the last. This shift in vantage points continues, again and again, revelation upon revelation of incomparable beauty, vision upon vision, until I am dizzy with the ecstasy of it all.

"Ishmel," I manage to whisper his name in the midst of my stupor. "I never realized . . ." A new formation of intergalactic star stuff returns me to my former state of speechlessness.

"Yes, Darling One."

I find my voice. "It seems to go on *forever*."

"Because it is forever eternal: space beyond space. Do you understand, Darling One?"

Now, without warning, the Bear dives, and we cut downward through it all at a speed so fast it seems as though we aren't moving at all. He lands, smooth, even, onto the grass in front of the lake. It is well past dawn, and sunshine filters onto us through the hazy pink of the morning sky. "Now, look around at this place, Darling One, and tell me what's happening."

I am not sure what to say.

"Start with the obvious. Describe what you see," he suggests.

"Okay. I see the lake surrounded by trees, and flowers I didn't notice before. They're lovely, yellow. Maybe they're daisies."

"Continue, Darling One. Move into physical sensations. But again, stick with the concrete, the obvious."

"Well, the sun overhead sure feels good on my neck."

"What else? What do you hear?"

"The water is making a gurgling sound, almost as if there were a waterfall on the other side, but I've been there and that's impossible. *Wait, I see you, on the bank on the other side!* But you were just right next to me. How did you do that?"

I hear the echo of his breath, loud from across the lake. And then, I feel it on the back side of my neck. I turn and link eyes with him beside me again.

"Remember this. I'm here with you always."

"But . . ."

"Everywhere, yes, but here, with you, for all time."

"How is that possible?"

"Look at the doorway to the lodge, Darling One."

"Well, it's brown, ordinary. It looks like someone made it from slats of wood."

"Really look at it."

"That's all I see. Is it symbolic of something?"

"Yes."

I look at him, still confused.

"What is inside is outside is inside and back again."

"I'm sorry, Ishmel. I don't get it."

"Always go back to the obvious. What do you see and hear right here, right now?"

"Water in the lake beside us. The sound of this unseen waterfall. You on the other side, but also right here. Is it something about the Source?"

"Good. Now look again at the doorway."

"The doorway goes into self? The meaning is something like: go into yourself, and . . . oh help, Ishmel."

"Okay. You did well. Go into yourself, into the seat of consciousness. Feel the ever-flow of me, all of it, and then light will emanate from above, through, in you.

"The Great All is never ending; it pulsates with energy you can ride, and time as you know it, Darling One, is an imaginary construct."

I am shivering. The image of Ishmel across the lake is gone. He has disappeared from beside me also.

I walk back to my tent. Exhausted and exhilarated, I curl into a ball inside my bag, and with the sun streaming through the flaps, I fall into the deepest sleep.

Chapter 1

PRECEPT TWO:

Time Is an Illusion

I WAKE IN THE AFTERNOON and decide to venture into the bath house sauna. It is warm and toasty in there, and when I pour water over the rocks, it becomes steamy. I allow myself to lie back and sweat while I consider my flight on Ishmel's back with the Raven by my side. That is when a beautiful woman enters. It has been so long since I've seen anyone at all that I jump.

"Oh, sorry," she apologizes.

She has long black hair down to her waist, and giant round eyes the same color. She is rather compact but regal in stature. The most distinctive feature about her is her tattoos. They cover her legs and travel most of the length of her belly, then down her arms and back. At first they seem like snakes on her legs, but then I realize I am looking at caterpillars. They curl into a cocoon on her belly before blossoming into butterflies of various shades at the top of her body. The entire effect is not messy, as you might expect, but delicate and intriguing.

"I'm camping alone," she offers. "By the lake."

"So am I." I try not to stare as she positions herself on the top board of the sauna. Something about her is distinctly familiar.

"I flew in yesterday," she volunteers. "Nothing like a good air trip."

"Your flight was smooth?"

"Oh, I wouldn't say that. The bumps were the best part. They really get the oxygen flowing." I like the broadness of her smile as she speaks. I think back to Ishmel and the Raven, how fun it was to soar over the forest, and yes, the bumps were the highlight.

"I'm Sherry." She holds out her hand, and when I take it, her long fingernails claw me.

"Sorry about that. I keep forgetting to clip them."

Again I have the distinctive feeling I know her from somewhere.

She leans back into the steam from the rocks. "So, are you having fun with Ishmel?"

I sit up. "You know Ishmel?"

"Who doesn't? I mean, he's kind of hard to miss."

She stands, wraps herself in her towel, and reaches for the sauna door.

"But, I thought . . ." I start.

"You think you're the only one," she finishes. "Everybody thinks that in the beginning."

She exits the sauna, leaving me to sit there alone, miffed. I plan to wait until I hear the door to the outside close, signaling her departure. Instead of the banging of the door, I hear the beating of wings inside the bath house. I leave the sauna to discover the Raven trapped inside. She beats her black wings against the window.

How careless Sherry was, I muse. She must have let the bird in by mistake when she left.

I open the door, and the Raven lunges out into the open space. She takes back to the skies, circling with her loud *whoo hoo* noises, before flying off to some mysterious point in the distance.

All day I circle the lake trails searching for Sherry's campsite, but find nothing. I begin to doubt her existence; maybe I dreamed her. In my mind, I review her comments about Ishmel, about how *everyone* thinks they're the only one in the beginning, and feel a tinge of irritation. Who is everyone? I hadn't seen anyone but Jerry and the odd hermit woman from the cave. Meanwhile, the loud *whoo hoo* of the Raven continues overhead. I wish I had an off button for the bird. I feel a nasty headache come on and lie down inside the tent. Even inside, the noise of the Raven is inescapable.

That night I sit in my usual spot on the log, ready to grill Ishmel with questions. By the time he finally arrives, later than usual, I am in a dither.

"Have you had a chance, Darling One, to contemplate the concept of time?" he asks.

I kiss him gingerly on the nose, and even tonight—when I am effectively annoyed with him—I feel my heart race at his presence. I tell myself to stop it. He is, after all, a bear, but I cannot control the undeniable quickening of my pulse or the creeping blush up my cheeks. Even though he appears as a bear, I cannot help but visualize him internally as a handsome Blackfoot warrior.

His blue-green eyes twinkle at my blush, but I refuse to be cajoled out of my fury. My physical reactions to his presence just make me angrier.

"Who's Sherry?" I launch into the issue.

"Sherry?" He pauses at length before managing, "Oh yes, you did meet her."

"Yes. In the sauna, but then how do *you* know that?"

"Oh, is that where it was?"

"She told you, didn't she? You saw her today, before me. Is she some sort of spy?"

"Darling One, you met her before today," he starts.

"I've never met her before. And anyway, she doesn't like me," I insist.

"It's not for lack of love that she circles you, but to wake you. You must admit she has an interesting perspective on things, up where she is."

"*Circles* me?" Then it hits: black hair, the fingernails so long they scraped me like talons, the compactness of her frame, and the mysterious appearance of the Raven in the steam room.

Sherry *was* the Raven. The Raven transformed into the beautiful woman she would be if she were human. I gulp.

"It's nice to fly like we did yesterday," Ishmel says. "You can see everything without any of the restraints of gravity."

"Yes," I agree. "It is nice."

"So, back to the concept of time. You realize now it is entirely man-made."

"How does time relate to our ability to fly around like that? Isn't being able to fly more related to space than time?"

"But they are the same. Where you place yourself spatially determines whether you reverse time, speed it up, or stop it altogether. Time is entirely relative, as science has already proven. It's smart to stop and be with the present moment. Then you see time as a construct of humanity, a device for marking minutes, hours, and days on clocks and calendars, nothing more. It's all happening at once, Darling One, this moment, every moment leading up to this moment, and every moment after it, going into infinity. The trick is to sit still."

"So, are you saying there's no reality?"

"Reality exists," he clarifies. "We are in fact part of that reality. We exist and morph. Time is an artificial measuring stick we've attached to morphing to avoid facing the hugeness of the concept that the current reality is all there is. Time, in the traditional sense, is a bit of a joke. *It's* the illusion, and modern scientists along with more and more modern philosophers are realizing that."

"But what about age? You can't deny the lines I've watched appear on the faces of my mother, my father, all those I love as time goes by."

"Appears to go by."

"Whatever. The aging process seems pretty inevitable to me, and it seems to prove that time exists."

"Aging is a form of morphing self. Morphing form within the present space. It proves nothing but that ability to morph, and it happens as different aspects of the infinite play out specific functions in space. Form becomes function in an instant, all within the continuum of present space."

I groan, "What's a continuum?"

"Picture an ant climbing a tree. The ant keeps crawling up the trunk. From its limited perspective as an ant on a tree, it feels like it has control of its own fate, like it could veer slightly to the right or left and design its own future. But really, despite its lack of understanding, despite its inability, unbeknown to it, to go anywhere but upward, it always ends up the same place it would have anyway, at the top of the tree. You see, there is no choice, just the trunk and the ant will always be there on the tree moving up or down or around and around it."

"I don't know, Ishmel. Eventually someone or something will come along and smash that ant, and then where does it end up? Smashed on a tree trunk."

"Nothing can ever really smash the ant because nothing really exists off the tree trunk. It may feel like it's been smashed for a moment, but actually it's just sort of smashed itself."

"What the heck?"

"By resisting, you see. By resisting its own fate to crawl up the tree. Too much resistance stifles the ant."

"Your analogy confuses me."

"Look at it this way. Every once in a while, humans get into a funk, a mood that prevents them from moving forward through their day. They might trip over the carpet or bang into someone else's car or argue with their spouse or parents or bruise themselves on the same furniture over and over again or walk into a tree branch, or—"

"I get it, Ishmel. We humans call it waking up on the wrong side of the bed."

"You've experienced this phenomenon, yes?"

"Yes. The day I decided to come here I fought with my boy-friend, and everything else went wrong, too."

"Of course. Human grief always comes in waves of resistance."

"Resistance? What do you mean by that?"

"Conflict—with the natural flow, with the course of destiny, with movement on the large trunk that is infinity. Let me ask you, when you argued with your boyfriend, did you feel resistance, any inner turmoil, about the course you took?"

"Yes. Tremendous conflict. I'm feeling it even now. I'm not sure if I did the right thing, leaving for the entire summer. Part of me wanted to stay with him, ignore my impulse to camp. Part of me is still angry at him. I mean, why couldn't he see how dissatisfied I was in L.A.? I feel almost as if I push things a bit. I might change him, tweak the situation so we can be together right now, happy, but of course I know deep down that won't work. It makes me miserable, and then I remember the sex, and I think the sex is so great when we're together, maybe we were meant to stay that way even though it makes me miserable. I'm confused."

"Yes, I see that. It's as if you're banging your head against the tree trunk itself, against infinity, against nature, and that causes pain. You're in there pounding against yourself, and it hurts. The argument you just described is an excellent example of resistance.

"Your head, when resistance happens, is full of possible scenar-ios that aren't currently present—asking 'What if?' and 'Should I?' and wondering 'Maybe later.' These imaginary scenarios pull you off the continuum and cause pain. From that place of pain, you become acutely aware of time passing, but you must understand it's not real. You're playing a mental game with yourself that is not useful at all. Time in that sense is a joke. You must understand, it's not passing at all. You're just stuck on the same point of that tree trunk, circling around and around, but getting nowhere."

Chapter 8

Time and Death

I POINT TO THE THREE little wrinkles on my forehead. "These are real enough, aren't they? They weren't here before. They just popped into existence after my fight with Brian. They prove time affects me."

Ishmel smiles. "No, Darling One. They prove your own ability to morph your physical being with resistance."

"You're right, of course. Maybe I am causing my own wrinkles, my own aging. Don't you get it? It's because I'm scared in the end. Terrified."

"Of?" The Grizzly knows the answer already. As usual, he wants me to say it myself.

I formulate the words to him. "Death. My end. Because age is the beginning of it, the dying. I know that feels shallow, but it's real, of course. No one wants an old shriveled hag. So all of us, women especially, have to do everything, anything to remain young and beautiful, or we're no good to anyone, see? But of course we can't help it—we have to get old in the end. Look at my mother. She had a face-lift a couple years ago, but it's worn off now. Eventually we all have to get old and die. It's not like we have a choice."

"Don't you, then?"

"Oh, I agree with what you're suggesting in theory, that age is simply a matter of resistance, but eventually people do resist. We can't help it; we're very frightened."

"But if you weren't frightened, do you think you would still age and die?"

"We *have* to age and die in the end."

"Why?"

"Because time goes by."

"Does it then? I thought I just explained about the whole time concept, didn't I?"

"What are you saying, Ishmel?"

"That since time is essentially a joke, you don't have to die, at least not in the traditional sense."

"The traditional sense? I didn't realize there was any other sense when it comes to dying."

"Darling One, you cannot leave life even if you want to. Instead, people morph by choice out of a body that has become too painful to inhabit any longer. So you morph to somewhere else. But even the concept of somewhere else is a joke. From your limited perspective, stuck on your particular circle going round and round the tree trunk, you've misdirected your energy, allowed yourself to spin, useless."

"But why would we do that?"

"You stated why yourself. Out of fear."

"But, if we weren't spinning like that, moving round and round in a fake circle that goes nowhere like you just explained—where would we be?"

"Where do you think, Darling One?"

"I don't know. Are you saying we can somehow get off the tree altogether?"

"The word you're looking for is *transcend*."

"Now I'm confused. What's the difference between *ascension* as in the ant up the tree, and *transcendence* as in Jesus or Buddha or someone like that?"

"Transcendence happens inside a person, and it has to do with stopping pre-conditioned mental habits, getting the mind to shut up long enough to be aware of what's really happening."

"What does that sort of transcendence have to do with the ant, and whether or not he's going up the tree?"

"The process of waking up is internal, a recognition of the tree and all of what you think is real as a mental construct. But until you are able to let the prior misconception of that tree dissolve and allow yourself to exist as the full reality of what it is—beyond the tree, but also *as* the tree in its full glory—it is appropriate to view the ant, liberated from his agonizing march around the trunk, in a state of pure ascension, a freedom that will ultimately allow it to transcend the limits of the hypothetical tree altogether. The time-space continuum is all just a matter of perception. You're always right here because there is nowhere else for you to go."

"Say again?"

"Heaven is earth, earth is heaven. Here is here is here is All There Is, All There Will Be, All There Ever Was. And every being on the planet already knows that to some extent."

"But the idea of heaven seems so different from living on earth. We're constantly involved in solid, practical, earthly activities in our lives here."

"Such as?"

"Making love or paying bills or earning money. They don't do those things in heaven."

"I tell you, Darling One, heaven and earth are one and the same. So when you 'die' there is nowhere for you to go but here, where you are already."

"Forget about dying for a moment, Ishmel."

"Good—because there's no such thing anyway."

"Yeah, okay, so you say. When I meditate or pray, it feels like I'm crossing some great divide, entering somewhere entirely different from my normal day-to-day life. When I meditate I feel, I don't know, more sacred than when I chop carrots, for instance. Now are you suggesting that I'm as close to heaven when I'm chopping carrots as when I pray?"

"Yes. At times you may even be closer when you chop carrots."

"What?"

"The sense that there are two planes of existence, that which is heavenly and that which is the earthly 'normal' life is untrue. Part of the space-time joke is that heaven is right here, right now, right where you are, within you. That's the magic. You, all of you, now, here, sit in heaven. It just a matter of realizing it.

"If you don't believe me, go do something that makes you feel alive—run through wet grass at night and look at the moon, let a lover whisper in your ear, feel his living breath, nourish your senses by taking in the sounds and colors of nature, a forest, a seashore, a misty valley. Live life, that's the secret. Dip deeply into life, and you'll discover the keys to heaven, to all eternity."

"But what of hell then?"

"There is no such place. What you term hell is simply anti-life."

"Death then?"

"No, I said before there is no death. There is, however, a state at which humans disengage from life, refuse to be involved, remain unaware, and they . . ."

"Is that when they resist?" I thought of Ishmel's prior explanation as to how people become stuck. I also thought of my own existence back in Los Angeles, with all my rushing around never getting me anywhere.

"Yes, excellent. Resistance eventually leads to separation—the state where one cannot connect with life."

"But it feels so separate, the physical world and the spiritual one. I tend to lose patience in my regular, earthly world—rushing around, clinging to people and material objects. The meditation helps. It sweeps me clean in a way. The days I don't meditate, I feel worse, so it must be the meditation, that drifting into another place, that's making me sane and loving."

"You're correct in the sense that meditation looks like it bridges the gap between a higher, transcendent plane and a ground level. Meditation certainly helps you to hook into a mind-set that lets you navigate appropriately through the physical world—yes, but you must realize there is no difference between your meditative state and your regular daily state. Realize that you can be in a meditative state, hooked up to heaven, all day, every day. Once that realization occurs, you will see the physical world for what it is—life manifested, All There Is, heaven, right here, right now."

Divinity in the ordinary. I love the sound of that, but I remain skeptical. So much of life seems full of fluff—actions or activities that don't seem to matter much—like putting gas in the car or feeding the cats or fussing around over people or events that don't seem to have meaning.

• *August 10, 2008*

I've met Ishmel three more times already today. We're still discussing time and divinity, and his response is always the same: search for divinity in supposedly simple activities and events. It's easier in dealings that involve people. "You'll find the divinity in their eyes, and then you'll quickly realize how much in common you have with all of them. Then all your daily chores will become divine. Let go into what you are doing—remember resistance causes wrinkles, and then bit by bit, you'll truncate time. You'll realize that it's all the same moment and the same space anyway, and all of it—in that magic instance is quite divine. Slow down just a bit and you'll realize that divinity."

I stop my mental talking at this point to notice just how peaceful the forest is, and how peaceful that peace makes me, and I feel thankful to Ishmel the Grizzly Bear despite the oddness of the situation and despite myself.

I know as I sit here by the lake that he is right about time. I've noticed it before of course—time going slower or faster depending on my own internal state, and I am very aware now that this moment, in all of its singularity, is really all there is.

I'm not certain how I get back into my tent to sleep. The Bear, Ishmel, walks with me for a bit, then retreats just before I reach the tent. It looks like he fades into the fog that surrounds me at that point. All I know is that when I wake up the next morning, light streams through the slits of the tent and I feel at peace.

Chapter 9

No Fear

BRIAN SHOWS UP, AND EVERYTHING shifts. He appears at noon as I write in my journal by the lake. My first reaction when I see him pull his car next to my rental in the empty dirt lot is relief. I shut my notebook and race for his car like a child.

Then I notice his face, pinched with worry, and I am reminded of why I've questioned my relationship with him in the first place. Brian always seems weighed down by fear. His focus during the three years I've known him has been material success. A main discussion point between us is how his current film is doing at the box office, important stuff if you work in Hollywood. He often refers to getting ahead in a vague manner that irritates me; I'm not sure whom we are always trying to surpass, nor do I understand why we want to be ahead of them in the first place. I mean, would anything so horrible happen if we were to just wait in the back of the hypothetical line?

Now, standing next to Brian in the lot, the gateway to the forest, I realize that what really bugs me about his go-get-'em attitude is its reflection of my own subconscious view of the world. I have to admit that I too feel an underlying sense that I must push to get the goodies in life. I'd be lying to myself if I didn't admit that Brian's whole survival-of-the-fittest routine, and his resulting success in the L.A. film scene, didn't attract me. Part of the reason I've fallen for Brian in the first place is my sense that he is an up-and-coming producer with clout, a practical man who will ultimately support me in a fairly affluent manner. I guess I'm okay knowing this about myself. I'm just not sure where Brian might stand with me once I let go of this extraneous and admittedly shallow attraction.

I also wonder what attracts him to me. I suppose I'm pretty by male standards, but if he wanted, he could easily find sex, or even a relationship, with a pretty woman back in L.A. without having to deal with my spiritual angst. I sense that our connection is based on something more intrinsic than mutual egotism; something amorphous holds us together. If I believed in reincarnation, I would suspect that we have been through many previous lives together. Something remains unresolved between us, and it is this lack of resolution that pulls us together, while at the same time stirs up conflict.

We hug, then kiss deeply. When we finally pull apart, Brian takes in the empty lodge and the overgrown lawn in front of the lake. "What is this place?"

"I'm not sure. Some sort of abandoned Blackfoot meeting place, I think."

"Is this really a good idea, honey?" he asks. I feel the unexpressed conflict floating wordlessly between us now. "Should you be camping like this on private property?"

"It's part of the National Forest." I tighten defensively. "Jerry, the man who works for the Forest Service, said it's okay."

"I don't know, honey."

"Look, I've been out here over a month. It's fine."

He pops open the trunk. "You've got to be getting bored with the whole camping in the woods thing by now."

"Why would you think I'm bored? I'm relaxing out here." I stop short as I notice the contents of his trunk. There, wedged between his suitcase and a sleeping bag, is a long hunting rifle.

I stop breathing. "What's *that* for?"

"Protection." With that, he shoulders the rifle and his suitcase. I carry his sleeping bag and lead him to my campsite.

• *August 11, 2008*

I can't seem to unpack my feelings about Brian. What is he doing here? I'd like to tell him about Ishmel, but he'd never believe me. He always says I'm far too vulnerable to the power of suggestion. It's patronizing, really, the way he downgrades my enthusiasm.

Brian is a man of logic; he wears it like a badge. I don't know why he's showed up with a gun. I don't know who or what he expects in the forest, but I know he's afraid of something.

Brian is familiar with the effects of fear from his job; he's worked for the past eleven years for a producer responsible for a slew of horror movies—Hollywood's latest master of psychological terror. Brian loves scary movies, not the type where someone gets chopped up by an ax murderer, but more subtle thrillers where someone's own worst mental fears come true. The unsettled ghost of a murdered father might come back to haunt the main character. In his guilt he must open his mind to a cannibalistic killer to save a life. A larger power with evil intentions always appears in such tales, and the viewers along with the character in the film realize they will never escape its clutches.

Brian's studio has amassed a small fortune in ten years of making films that prey on these fears. Now as he enters my campsite with the rifle over his shoulder, I consider that the gun's a fake, something he picked out of a Hollywood sound stage. He's just posing as a hunter, like one might do for Halloween.

I walk back to my campsite, where I catch Brian shooting, Butch Cassidy-like, a 7-Up can on a rock. This feat is not as impressive as it sounds. He stands three feet away, and it takes him five tries to shoot down the can. I realize the gun is real.

"You don't actually expect to use that on anything alive?" My words are more an admonishment than a question.

"There are lots of dangerous animals out here. I read about them on the net."

"Dangerous? Like what?"

"Grizzly bears, for one. They stalk menstruating females. It's true."

"Come on, Brian. All that stuff about don't camp during your period—it's nonsense."

"Grizzlies eat humans. I read all about it."

The irony of a man who produces films about psychological monsters standing before me with a rifle, ready to aim at a man-eating grizzly, does not escape me. I pray that Ishmel will stay away now that Brian and his ridiculous rifle have joined me.

"Put that thing down," I demand in frustration, and much to my relief he lowers the gun and clicks on the safety latch.

Brian is the consummate L.A. boy; his camping skills consist of whatever paltry memories he can drum up from a Boy Scout camp he attended in the fifth grade. Considering he is now in his thirties, his tromping into the Helena forest to save me with a rifle he'd be lucky to even aim properly strikes me as silly. I laugh at the ridiculousness of the situation, and thankfully he joins me.

Fear involves telling stories. Sometimes the stories are happy, but they must always be exciting. Storytelling, after all, thrives on conflict. So there is a certain seduction in the thought of Brian, my long-lost lover, heroically saving me from harm. Never mind that his rifle was a spontaneous purchase at an army surplus store with a quickly procured license. Never mind that Brian can't aim, despite a two-day crash course hitting targets in the desert by Lancaster he says he just completed.

We are, all of us, seduced by our own funny little fear stories. So when Brian tells me the recent earthquake I'd felt was not an earthquake at all but underground bomb testing by terrorists—bad guys hidden in some tunnel in nearby mountains—I have no choice but to stop laughing. He believes what he believes, and I don't argue.

"There's something extremely valuable in this forest," he suggests. "The extremists are out to get it at all costs."

"What 'treasure' could be sitting out here in the middle of nowhere?"

"It's not clear. According to the experts in the *Times*, it's something extremely powerful."

Fear of failure, fear of success, fear of the mugger down the street, fear of my potential mother-in-law, sister-in-law, cousin, lover, husband. Fear of earthquakes that aren't earthquakes, wars that only exist on some esoteric level on the other side of the planet, starvation, sleeplessness, deprivation, injury, boredom, over-excitement, lack of love, friendships that aren't friendships, rejection by peers. Fear of motherhood, aging without love or without adventure, aging in general. Fear of terrorists that aren't really terrorists. Afraid of you, me, everyone, but most of all, afraid of fear.

All these fears that engender more fear; fear upon fear upon fear until we're buried under it—layer upon layer of smothering, proliferating, merciless fear. It sucks us dry in the end, because the irony remains that every fear we've ever had, every fear we ever *will* have, is destined to come to complete fruition if only because we created it in the first place, nurtured it, bathed in it, held out our hearts to it as if to say, "I'm so scared, it's unbearable, so you can have me, fear, because I can't stand it anymore." And it consumes us bit by bit, tearing off little pieces of ourselves until we are unrecognizable.

It is fear that leads me to lie next to Brian that night, let him peel off my sweats and make love to me. My mind drifts to the Grizzly during all of it. Ishmel floats through dream upon dream in the form of a bear, then a man.

I tell myself it's not important, that my thoughts of the Bear mean nothing, but I know that's a lie. I tell myself I'm just getting off on having a secret from Brian, that it really is only Brian I care about, but that is a lie too. I don't want so many lies in my life.

I wonder what it feels like to die. Do people give in to their unconscious lies about life when they make their exit? Is it because they're playing a game with the truth? Maybe they just decide life hurts too much to stick around. What would be the name of such a game—Death, Disease, Suffering, or This Sucks, See You Later?

I wonder about the story of Lazarus—the one in which Jesus raises someone from the dead. I wonder how he could have done that. Maybe Lazarus was always alive; maybe Jesus didn't do anything special at all in that story. Maybe he just noticed the truth.

I slip into a dream about Ishmel the man. We are collecting branches to fuel a fire for this Blackfoot sweat lodge. It looks like a small igloo in the center of the forest. There are other people from a tribe, his tribe, there, adding fuel to the fire outside. Ishmel offers me his hand. I am afraid initially because the enclosure is so small, but I can refuse him nothing.

We are naked inside the sweat lodge. The fire makes a hissing noise from outside as the people pile on the wood, seal us inside the steamy darkness. The thickness of that steam burns my eyes. I feel Ishmel's calloused hands, rough from manual labor, in mine.

"I know this is scary, Darling One, but be relaxed, be soft. All is well." His words come into my mind as they do when I commune with Ishmel the Bear during my waking hours.

It is so dark in the sweat lodge that other than his hand in mine, I feel completely alone in that steamy, locked-in place. I am sweating now—it beads uncontrollably all over my body. His hand slips away from mine. I am trapped in there, in that dark place where everything purifies itself.

I sense Brian's arms, not as muscular as Ishmel's, around me. Brian holds my slippery body. What is Brian doing here, in my dream, in this private space I share with Ishmel? I attempt to scream, but the air is so thick around me that I am unable to inhale enough of it to make a noise. I was suffocating before, but now I am aware of cold air all around me. I sit up from my dream, drenched in sweat.

Brian pulls me back down, next to him, "Shhh, you were dreaming." I allow him to snuggle me spoon-like, close, but in my mind it becomes Ishmel, not Brian, who holds me.

I whisper my love for the Grizzly to his Bear form, then to his Human form, then to other indefinable forms he assumes in my dream. He brushes his silver hood to my lips and whispers back to me, "Let go of all fears. That is the Third Precept, Darling One: Have no fear."

• *August 18, 2008*

Brian stayed a week. Each night, he sat in the tent, nervous and uncomfortable. He's always hated camping. He'd cock his rifle and aim out into the woods, ready to annihilate any predator or terrorist that might disturb us. When he would finally disarm, put down his weapon, we'd make love.

The day before he left, we had a fight. He said he understands why I am tired of working as a school teacher, so he's arranged a job for me in casting, something I've always wanted to do. I'm always matching actors, and sometimes non-actors, with parts in the movies we see together. I have a knack for finding the real, living, breathing characters locked inside other people, and Brian knows it. My old desire to work in casting was our topic of conversation at the party where we first met. The thing that stuck out about Brian at that party was the giant fish tie he wore, an anomaly for an up-and-coming Hollywood producer. It's been three years since then, but only one since he's been pushing the marriage question. I like Brian all right; he is a competent lover and kind most of the time. I'm just not sure he's the man I want to marry. *Usually our fights involve marriage, or rather my lack of interest in the subject.*

Our fight this time took a new turn. Brian didn't understand why I wouldn't jump at this position he's found for me; the pay is twelve times what I make as a math teacher.

I said no to the casting job over and over again. Brian wanted me to leave the forest right then, go home with him, and again I refused.

"How can you just sit out here doing nothing all summer? You're burning through all your savings."

I told him I don't need much out here, and I still have plenty of savings.

"But what about your career? What about us?"

I didn't have the heart to tell him I wasn't sure about either one.

Brian was covered with mosquito bites from his week out here. We both knew he would leave with or without me in the morning.

I did impress him with my ability to make soup out of the funny, flat-edged mushrooms that grow around the campsite. As I waved goodbye I knew he couldn't get past my lack of ambition. I also knew I am neither free of him nor of Los Angeles.

Brian is a good man. Part of the problem is his desperate love for me without knowing who I am. It frightens me, makes me restless. Had he stayed in my tent even one more hour, I would have left with him. Brian smothers me as no one else can. I look forward to a long visit from Ishmel tonight.

Chapter 10

The Spider's Web

INSTEAD OF SEEING ISHMEL, I become ill. My stomach churns, and I start to wonder about the wild mushroom soup I prepared last night. How stupid I must be to have prepared a soup from the strange floppy-edged mushrooms growing wild by my tent. I thought I was being so accomplished, demonstrating my high-level wilderness skills by making a soup only from forest ingredients. The reality is, even when in Los Angeles—one of the largest, most thorough cities for culinary supplies in North America—I am a lousy cook. I can't cook to save my life. Here in the forest, my cooking is tantamount to suicide. I know that now.

As I vomit the contents of my digestive tract again and again, until there is nothing left to regurgitate except air, and later blood. I take comfort in the fact that if I am sick from the wild mushroom soup, Brian must also be ill. I want Brian to suffer just as much as I am. Even as I realize such a thought is wrong, I can't help thinking it. Misery loves company, I tell myself.

I curl in a ball on the floor of my tent. I try to relax, take deep breaths. When I do, I cough up another mound of phlegm and blood. This time the blood seems darker than before. I realize I am all alone.

I dehydrate. I know I dehydrate because all the things that typically happen to people who dehydrate happen to me. I am dizzy. I feel weak. I cannot stand. I focus on a black Spider as she weaves a web in the corner of my tent, and wonder how I could have missed her until now. She is beautiful, this Spider. She is sure of herself. If I watch her long enough, I can actually see her generate the web from the pit of her belly. I wonder if Spider webbing is a teachable skill and if she is fully conscious of her doings, or whether it is just an automatic reflex, sort of like breathing.

I lie there watching her for hours. She snags a fly, and for an instant, I pity the fly as she wraps it tightly up. Then I forget the fly's needs altogether in a wave of intense admiration of her. She is a true artist. The sides of the tent blur. I know I will die soon, alone, here in the woods.

"Ishmel!" I cry out for my Grizzly with a sense of desperation; but he does not appear. I know it is hopeless, that I can never demand his appearance that way. The universe simply won't have it. Instead, I must die. It is a simple matter of self-preservation. The universe must choose itself over my singular wants. The Grizzly will never appear when I demand him from a place of desperation, a place that insists on mere magic.

I close my eyes.

"You seek the Bear, of course." The voice I hear is undeniably female.

My eyes snap open to look the Spider in the eye. She is next to my face now, so I know it is her I hear. There is no one else.

"How long have you been here in the tent?" I manage to sputter from my parched lips. "Have you seen everything?"

She nods. It bothers me that the Spider has been watching me all along. She must have seen Brian and me make love, heard our fight, and watched me mix the wild, poisonous mushrooms that will kill us both. She must know that on some level I've betrayed Brian with the Grizzly. It is irritating, really.

I have always had issues with authority. I believe most people do, so while I admire the Spider's tenacity and skill with the web, acknowledging the astuteness of her observations, I am also annoyed at her position, however subtle, as an authority figure above me. She hangs literally above me now, dangling from a strand of her web.

"You know, Spider," I sputter as I inch closer and closer to death. "You saw me mix the mushrooms in the pot."

"Ah, yes," comes her reply. "That particular type of mushroom is, as you've now surmised, quite poisonous, fatal actually, when consumed by humans like yourself."

I groan, roll back into my ball, and wait for the end. I feel a rush of guilt and affection for Brian. I am dying, and I think of Brian. I love Brian. I've always loved Brian. I was only pretending before, when I didn't think it mattered, and now it is too late. I will die without him knowing my true feelings, and that will be a tragedy.

I sob—even as dehydrated as I am, the tears flow. I long for my mother. I don't tell her I love her often enough either. She wraps me in blankets when I am sick. Were she here, she could cure me with her love.

"There are other humans nearby, you know. Much closer in proximity than your mother." So, as I suspected, the Spider can read my mind. I watch her skillfully zip back into her web and bite into the fly, sucking away its life blood.

"No," I sob. "I am completely on my own out here. I made sure when I picked this site no one was around."

She laughs, and it resembles the tinkling of bells in a rattle. "Go to the man and the other woman. Their tent is only a few hundred yards from here. Next to the creek."

"What man and woman? There's no one. I told you. I've scouted this place, been all over."

"Go to the others. They may save you."

I curl deeper into my ball. "I can't move. It hurts."

"It's only a few hundred yards. By the creek."

I crawl most of the way. It takes over an hour, an excruciating, painful hour because my stomach doubles me over every couple of feet. Halfway there—on some wet leaves—I despair. Maybe the Spider lied for her own amusement. She is probably nearby, watching my agony with glee.

But when I look up, I see the unmistakable trail of smoke from a fire nearby. I inch toward the other campsite. It is not my will that gets me there alive, but rather my willingness. Slowly I allow the stubborn bits of my being that cling to the pain to release. When I stop clinging to all that is painful—my gut, my head, my supreme, resplendent loneliness—I manage to crawl in a daze to the newly pitched tent of Peter and Sophie.

Chapter 11

PRECEPT FOUR:

Release into Love

THEY ARE THE EPITOME OF a loving couple: Sophie and Peter. He is a nature photographer whose photos have appeared in *National Geographic* and *Montana Outdoors,* among many others. I love his tuft of sandy brown hair. His eyes are clear blue, and he is thin and chiseled from hiking to various locations, exotic and otherwise. I enjoy that most about him—the fact that he has been everywhere and that he sees the world so clearly through the penetrating lens of his camera. I don't even need to see his photographs to know that whatever he shoots is beautiful and true and revealing.

His jittery creativity is balanced by Sophie. It is her calm gaze I see first when I stumble toward their fire. Long blonde hair, thick eyelashes, heavy, brown eyes—all of her refreshingly earthy, anchored. I can trust Sophie. I lean against her instinctively, want to die in her arms if that is indeed my fate.

"I've eaten poisonous mushrooms," I manage before my eyes close, and I do collapse there with her holding me.

• *August 19, 2008*

I opened my eyes today, not to the forest, but to the sterile walls of St. Peter's Hospital in Helena. Peter and his wife, Sophie,

*saved me in the end. They gathered up my collapsed body and
rushed me here. The nurses gave me shots for food poisoning and
an IV for dehydration.*

*I've always hated hospitals. I hate the feeling of losing control
one experiences as one surrenders to nurses and doctors who may
or may not know what they are doing.*

*Yet I didn't have much choice last night. The nurse told me I
could have died. Now I'm flat on my back and staring at the
ceiling above me. I feel intense gratitude for being alive.*

"Oh, you're awake." Sophie's voice is soothing and grounded after
my recent psychic conversations with the Spider.

"Brian . . ." In an instant, I remember the damage I might have
done, stunned that early in my suffering I wanted Brian to suffer
too. My guilt is overwhelming, and I blink back a spontaneous rush
of tears.

"The man who keeps calling here," Sophie quickly responds.

"He's alive?"

"Yes—alive and well, and working on some blockbuster movie
in Los Angeles, from what I understand."

"He's not sick like me?"

"Not that I've heard. He's called here several times to check on
you."

"But we ate the same thing—the mushrooms—he has to be sick."

"I don't know. Maybe you're not sick from mushrooms after all."

"No. It's the mushrooms. It has to be the mushrooms."

• *August 20, 2008*

*I realized with Sophie's help that unless I surrendered, released
into what was happening to me, I would suffer. Peter's presence
helped too, but he didn't come by as often to visit, and he seemed
awkward when Sophie did leave me alone with him. Peter*

*reminds me of my father; he cares enough, but he doesn't quite
know how to show it, and he certainly doesn't want to talk
about it.*

I can't stop vomiting the contents of my stomach even when there
are no contents left. I vomit nothingness—my own nothingness—
as if my body is expunging itself of all resistance. My fears, forgotten in my mind lifetimes ago, are embedded to such an extent in my
psyche that releasing them is a momentous event.

I lie in that hospital bed and wonder if I will die from the shock
of it all. I am stiff, so very stiff, and I miss my mother, but dare
not worry my parents with a phone call. I think often of Ishmel. I
know he cannot come bodily into the hospital room in Helena; he
is a creature of the forest. So I sink into despair. My fear of abandonment by everyone I love weighs heavily on me. But whenever I
think of giving up, of dying, Sophie appears with a knowing smile
and pulls me back into life.

- *August 24, 2008*

*The doctors determined that it was indeed the mushrooms that
made me sick. I decided to cooperate with them and allow myself
to heal. Instead of stiffening my way into nothingness, I released
into love.*

*It started with Sophie. I let her brush out my hair when I could
sit up in the hospital bed without retching. Eventually, I also
accepted her hugs.*

*Sophie told me she had been deathly ill the year before with an
unexplained bout of Lyme disease. She knows what it is like to
lie for an undefined amount of time in St. Peter's hospital.*

*I've stopped pushing away the medication and the food that my
nurses present to me. I take all they offer willingly now.*

• August 26, 2008

*Today I left the hospital. Peter took a series of photos of me in
my hospital gown. I hated those pictures at first, but I've learned
to cherish them. There is an element of peace in my face that
wasn't there before; my previous tense expression is gone.*

*I decided not to tell my parents about my foray in the hospital.
I know if they heard, they would talk me into coming home.
Instead, I returned to my tent and campsite, still right where I'd
left them two weeks earlier, thanks to Peter—who's incorporated
checking in on my stuff, and sweeping out my tent, into his daily
routine.*

*I am glad of the presence of Peter and Sophie so close down
the path from me. I dined with them tonight, the first night of
my return. When we finished the fresh trout Peter had caught
from the stream, I made my way back to my waiting tent slowly,
stopping often to look up at the stars. They are so bright, it is
easy to write by starlight now.*

I sigh, put down the pen, and analyze those stars again. Was it really
possible that just a few weeks prior, I flew right through them?

I look back down and see Ishmel. He stands next to my tent. I
have no idea how long he's been there.

I am so happy to see him after the long absence in the hospital
that I cry soft tears. Despite my gladness, I feel strange with him
after the long separation.

I am nervous and excited all at once. My heart pounds in my
chest, and my first instinct is to run away. I'm not sure what I should
do. He suggests I make some tea, and as I sip from the steaming cup,
we discuss my sickness and recovery.

"Why did the mushrooms poison me but not Brian?" I ask him.

"What is poisonous to one being can be supremely nutritious to someone else. It's not the food source so much as the mental process of digesting what enters the body. Words can be equally poisonous or nutritious depending on how we choose to 'digest' them."

"That doesn't sound very scientific," I argue.

"That's okay," the Bear explains. "It has actually been proven on more than one level by your scientists. The main cause of all illness is not a particular food or relationship or job, but stress from a blocked or unaware interaction. It becomes an issue of awareness."

"Are you saying we can eat anything?"

"If you let it digest properly. In the case of food, you should always realize its potential for imbuing life force into your body. You should hook up with that life force before you take it into yourself, and then as you consume it, be aware of your own processes. Let your food become a source of love and light, and it won't matter what you eat in particular. It is your awareness that determines whether you are healthy and vibrant, or ill and heavy."

"I get where you're going with this, Ishmel—I should establish a positive relationship with my food—but I didn't harbor any ill will toward the mushrooms when I ate them."

"Perhaps the genesis of your pain was your negative interaction with your Beloved One. The mushrooms just absorbed that negativity back into your body."

"My Beloved One?" I pause. "Are you saying I got sick because I fought with Brian? That's just stupid."

"Remember it is never the person or the food that sickens you, but your resistance to them. Energy, the life force, is constantly in motion. Your own issues—unresolved guilt, anger, depression—become smoke screens for the ego and cause pain. The stronger your resistance, the deeper your suffering."

This suggestion that I am responsible for my own suffering both annoys and intrigues me. "So it was me. I blocked my own life force. What exactly is that, anyway?"

"Love, Darling One. It is love."

"Oh."

"The key to all healing is to learn how to release into love."

I feel lighter when he says that.

Instead of returning directly to my tent, I walk back to my rental car. It is only a few miles' drive down the road, a short distance really, to the point where I can use my cell phone. I dial my parents. Mom answers, and her voice cracks with relief as we speak.

"Are you having a good time?" she asks.

"Sure, Ma. Everything's great."

"Your father will be so happy you called. He was getting worried."

"Is Dad okay?"

"He's in a holding pattern for now. Sorry, but he's asleep. I'll tell him you called."

"Thanks, Mom. I love you." With those few words, so much between us is resolved.

• *August 27, 2008*

Releasing into love requires the ultimate act of surrender—the ultimate letting go into what is. Fears have no place there. They stem from conflict about who you are and what you should be doing at any given time. Hidden guilt—contemptuous, deceitful hiding in your pores—prevents you from the release. It stiffens you, forces you to stand paralyzed right in front of what will save you, could you just take a small step forward. Instead you freeze like Percival, face to face with the Holy Grail, but not quite able to touch it.

It would be dishonest for me to say that I completely released upon Ishmel's explanation. I still worry that if I completely let go, I might turn into a zombie, or even worse, be abused and hurt. He did give me a new mantra though, and that's helped me to relax a bit. "Know yourself as the love that constitutes being." I'm not sure what exactly that means, but it makes me feel better to say it: I know myself as the love that constitutes being.

I keep repeating it. Somehow those words make me feel less tight, and then I feel loved by lots of people, not just Ishmel, but Sophie, Peter, Sherry, who I keep bumping into in the sauna, Brian, even my parents. I guess I wasn't really accepting their love before now. I've been holding myself tight, refusing to let go. I guess love and release work together.

Chapter 12

Communing with Ishmel from Anywhere

• *August 28, 2008*

I can communicate with Ishmel even when he is far away, in other parts of the forest. I ask him questions while I sit on my rock, and receive answers from him even when he gathers berries on the hill three miles away. He often sends me mental messages—loving ones always—and they are a source of comfort to me. I find myself answering them back mentally with gratitude.

I receive his mental messages more and more often. I am oddly familiar with his train of thought. I instinctively feel where he is and what he does throughout the day even if I do not see him in the flesh. I begin to suspect that he is more than what he appears to be, that perhaps I am also more than what I appear to be. Could his scope of influence over me through the channels of my mind be too great? What does it mean that I can communicate long distance mentally with a Grizzly Bear? I wonder if our form of communication is unique to the Bear and me, or whether other creatures engage in what seems to me a mystical form of speaking.

This recognition of Ishmel as containing the same life stuff as me is a huge revelation because it means I can ultimately become independent of the Grizzly. I tell myself that it will never happen, that Ishmel and I will be bodily together forever.

I begin to sense the colors of the forest in all their vibrancy. I tingle, and things glow around me for longer and longer intervals; and I've become used to the sensation of being connected to all of it. I remember Brian's face without its harsh edges. I begin to soften myself. As I soften, I notice myself more able to slide into a communion with the plants and animals around me. I realize there is more to the woods than I initially saw, and as a result, I tread more softly through it.

I sit often at the circular rock formation, but not because I grasp for visits from Ishmel. I sit so I can delve into my own silence and by degrees slip deeply into the silence of the living, breathing woods around me. I like my newfound sensitivity even as I realize it makes me much more vulnerable. It takes a certain degree of courage to open up that way, but in the end, it is worth it. It is always worth it.

• *September 3, 2008*

I'm sitting at the Helena airport waiting for my flight home as I write. As Brian predicted, my funds are depleted. I'm due back in Los Angeles tomorrow.

I lingered too long in the forest, waiting for one last visit from Ishmel. It never happened.

Peter helped me load my things into the car. It was hard to hug Sophie and Peter good-bye, but they are leaving for the winter anyway.

Chapter 13

Happiness vs. Joy

• *January 30, 2009*

Sorry to have not written in so long. I've missed it. I married Brian last month despite unresolved issues with Ishmel and the forest. We are happy together, but sometimes in my happiness, I feel a distinct lack of satisfaction. I realize that happiness is subtly but importantly distinct from joy.

Joy is often a matter of bravery. One might be on the brink of death, standing up for truth, and experience extreme joy. Joy comes when your heart so completely opens, you quiver. Joy squashes all fear by degrees and stands true to itself. Joy is capable of undergoing extreme discomfort. Joy will sacrifice its own happiness. Joy feels not complacent, but ecstatic.

As I live with Brian, I've become well acquainted with the joy/happiness paradox. Brian is a sweet man. He is an apt lover and a considerate roommate. He consistently picks up his socks, his books, and neatly deposits all his spare coins into a clearly designated change tray on our bureau. I adore him in most respects. Yet while I am quite satisfied in my happiness with him, our marriage lacks joy. I am okay with that. Lots of people are happy without joy, and they survive. Brian and I live in peaceful complacency, but in the back of my mind, I wonder about Ishmel and sense a great lack in my life.

I feel the lacking strongly at times, and at others I drown it out with chatter, the droning noise of my daily life, teaching, sorting mail, playing the role of wife to Brian. I suppose it is inevitable that as we reach a certain level of happiness, we yearn for joy. It cannot be ignored, this yearning. The yearning leads me to seek a second summer in those Montana woods.

• *July 1, 2009*

Brian was initially opposed to the idea of my returning to Montana. He never voiced his opposition outright. Instead, he asked about the practicality of my mission, inquiring about long underwear, bug repellent, and freeze-dried food. He reminded me repeatedly not to pick the wild mushrooms. But I was determined to go, so here I am again.

• *July 1, 2009, midnight*

My first night back in the woods, and all is peaceful. The giant sleeps, I suppose. I feel this incredible urge to telephone Brian, but of course, my cell phone won't work.

A strong feeling of peace comes over me in the morning as I walk the familiar trails, listen to the familiar sound of the wind on my tent. I realize just how much love I have back at home from Brian and my parents, such abundance. I am deeply grateful for what I have there.

As the sun goes down over the lake, ripples appear in the water as though it rains a soft rain, but that is not the case. I realize it is the fish leaping from under the depths of the water for insects on the surface. It is lovely; fish movements make reverse indentions on the lake's surface—the opposite of a pebble falling into water, inverted, a series of mini big bangs that expand into larger and larger circles. There are lots of these circles on the lake, fifty or more all expanding into the water over and over again. They are marvelous, really.

I watch this event in the late evenings just as the sun sets. The concentric circles are harder to see during the day, but I suspect, like the stars, they are still there.

• *July 2, 2009*

Twenty-four hours into my repeat experience in the woods, and nothing, no sign of the Bear at all.

I stir my habitual meal of baked beans over my fire and feel rightfully anxious. After all, Ishmel may just be playing games with me, a swat here or there, like what my housecat does to a mouse before she decimates it. Ishmel is, after all, a bear, a predator. Maybe I am nothing to him but a meal embodied. Perhaps he is just hungry, calling me back here to swat at me a bit for sport before gobbling me up, spitting out my bones, and then forgetting about me. That is, of course, my fear speaking. I am terrified of my possible renewed acquaintance with him; the thought of our reunion makes my heart feel utterly vulnerable and open.

• *July 5, 2009*

Day five in the woods and still no contact. I am actually getting a bit bored. I've listed items I need to pick up back in Helena: baked beans, flashlight batteries, bottles of water.

There are lifestyle choices that are tough for me here. I don't want to give up my Los Angeles existence altogether—dining out, the theater, facials—even in exchange for enlightenment. It is hard to let all these accoutrements go and head into the unknown for some undefined experience that may or may not matter to the rest of the world. I know I've planned on making this whole repeat adventure temporary. There's no way I'd be able to give up all the goodies of city life permanently. Still, I cursed the hardness of the ground when I tweaked my neck last night.

In the morning, my sixth day out here, I find Ishmel. He sits alone in his meadow—Bear Meadow, I call it—eating berries. I feel a bit annoyed that he does not run toward me. He glances up at my appearance but continues chewing without moving at all. I wonder if he is angry with me for leaving and staying away so long.

He sits up and stares at me when he finishes. I watch the juice run down the length of the gray hairs on his chin. For a split second, I think I made a mistake. Maybe this isn't him at all. Maybe I stand eye to eye with some other random bear.

After what must be the longest pause in my life, he responds to me mentally. "You've come back. Good to see you."

So begins my second summer with Ishmel in the Montana wilderness.

Chapter 14

The Creators and the Created

TODAY ISHMEL GIVES ME A lesson in creation. It begins with Raven. She heralds the lesson from a tree above with her usual *whoo hoo* sound, as though cheering us on from the bleachers. I pull on a tank top and shorts and head outside the tent, where Ishmel is waiting. Raven circles above us, making a striking image, her solid, black wings against the orange of the rising sun. She dives over the lake, around and through us, summoning all the magic of that place, awakening a creative force that sweeps over us like a crashing wave.

It is then that I become acutely aware of the Snake coiled below us. He prepares to strike. His shed skin lies inches away from him, evidence of his potency.

Now he reveals himself in all his dragon-like glory. He uncoils bit by bit, along the trail to the bath house. Has he been on this trail before, coming and going just like any other animal, unnoticed by me until now, or is this his first visit? He is so shiny and smooth, marvelously bendy.

I stand, Ishmel at my side, in awe of him. With that awe, all prior fear about this Snake, all snakes, drops away. He slithers toward me, stopping directly at my foot, an act of extreme bravery on Snake's part because I can easily stamp on his delicate head with my hiking boot.

We remain that way for a bit. I look down at him and am aware of the trepidation in the Snake as he looks up into my eyes. My body shudders with anticipation—quite different from fear—and the Snake's forked tongue flicks in and out of his mouth with perfect synchronization. He slithers around my ankle and moves his way up my bare leg. His body is less slippery than I imagined. It feels solid as it attaches to mine, and I can feel my own skin relax and conform to the Snake as I attach myself to him.

I let out a soft sigh and wait. The Snake moves up my leg to my groin, wraps around my lower belly, slithers across my navel to the left side of my chest, settling right over my heart. He settles there for a bit, and I sense the rhythm of his breathing, his tongue issuing in and out of his mouth. The beating of my own heart begins to coordinate to the Snake's movements. Beat, beat, beat, we vibrate as one for five minutes or so. Finally, the Snake slithers around my neck and stops to make contact with my throat before making his way over my lips, up between my eyes, to the crown of my head.

It is glorious then: the beating of my heart, my breath, my being merging with the Snake's movements, each nerve ending in my head stretching up to meet the Snake's head atop mine, my entire being straightening up and opening, allowing me to know as I never could know before what it means to be alive.

Now is the time for creation, now when the Snake has bounded up my being into my senses and taken over my pain. He holds my pain, cradles it, keeps it safe and silent until it absorbs into the atmosphere. This happens quickly and easily and with love.

The pain has been building up in me for so long. The Snake draws it up into my head, like a blemish full of pus. It has been waiting so long to be released that all it takes is a nudge from the Snake, the great dragon that he is, and it expels. I feel a grand opening from the top of my head downward, and an instantaneous release of my pain and everything that goes with it: guilt, judgments of self, judgments of others, anger, inner conflict, struggle.

The release is sweet and sudden. Once the pain is gone, there is so much more room for illumination. What I sensed before as simply a tiny crack, an opening in the veneer of suffering, is now a wide-open conduit for joy.

The tears come. They must come because the release is so significant. How long have I trudged through the world carrying the weight of this incredible pain? It has been longer than this singular lifetime, to be sure.

In answer to my personal release of tears, thunder rumbles in the cloudy sky, and heavy drops fall. I stand there, my arms outstretched, my chest open to the sky, and let myself get soaked. The Snake slithers up and down the length of my body. He tightens and loosens to match the small shudders my body makes as I cry. The rain pounds down harder and harder, and I remain standing on the trail with my heart wide open until I am completely soaked.

I relish this release. I realize the power inherent in this light. I feel Ishmel somewhere around me, but when I look for him, he appears only as a huge mass of light energy. The Snake on my body is light energy too, and now I see that without the weight of my earlier pain, I am also that selfsame light energy. I stare in awe at the current that runs through my fingers, up and around my arms.

A loud clap of thunder, louder than ever before, deafening. The loudness of it rattles my entire being, shakes the forest itself. I lose my footing, slip, and my face hits the trail that has become mud. Now the lightning hits again and again, in stronger and stronger bolts, closer and closer to where I lie. I turn my face toward the sky. Again and again the lightning strikes, like a giant camera flash over the earth. It fills the entire forest with violent, strong, powerful light. I sink to the ground.

The light around my body and the Snake's body becomes the light of the grass and the trees and the sky. Light, light, and more light. Rushes and rushes of light. Louder and louder thunderclaps. The rain pouring down, so strong, so heavy, so relentless that I can barely lift my head. The majesty of the light held back for so long under the pain asserts itself to me and the world in those flashes, and I remain cowered down, realizing how silly it was to ever think pain was a threat. I know now the pain was insignificant, a drop perhaps, a small indentation in the power ocean that composes the creative strength of the Great Light.

All hail the light! Let every being bow before the wonder and strength of its infinite glory. Hallelujah! Hallelujah! Illuminata! Rejoice now and always and for all time!

After my experience with the Snake, I stand much taller. It is as if I haven't been filling in the entire length of myself but never noticed it. I feel open and perceptive and true—naked, but not in an embarrassed, shrunken, withdrawn sense—naked in the sense of finally being completely liberated. My clothes are a burden to me at that point, the visible cover for the parts of me that are blocked. When the Snake liberates me, everything that was weighing me down, including my unnecessary clothing, dissolves.

Now I stand on the path, naked and alive and open, and I become aware of Ishmel standing there too. I understand how it is that he manages to communicate with me telepathically—even when I am far away from his current embodiment as a bear. Ishmel is always wide open, an enlightened one, so he can flit into my mind, and probably anyone else's mind, at will, provided the mind in question is sufficiently open to him.

I feel the sudden, undeniable urge to hug him, my emissary, my teacher, and now that I am open and free of impediments thanks to the Snake, any trace of fear I may have harbored on account of him being a Grizzly has dissipated. I walk toward him and take him in my arms, not minding his current embodiment as a Grizzly at all, enjoying it rather, the silver sparkle of hairs below his chin—the thickness and warmth of his fur.

He is a Grizzly to me because I have embodied him that way from the beginning. I myself have embodied him as a bear, just as he has shaped me into a woman. We have shaped and formed each other at will. We've created each other in our own eyes, and we are beyond pleased. I stay with him a long time that way, curled up in the soft cradle of his chest—Ishmel the wonderful, Ishmel the terrible, Ishmel, my love.

When finally we roll apart, we laugh. His is a rumble from deep within his soul. That is when we begin the lovely process of re-creating everything around us just as you, dear reader, will re-create that perfection which surrounds you. Let go of your burdens then. Shed them as the Snake sheds its uncomfortable shell when it weighs too heavily. Shed the heaviness of all those burdens, passed down from self to self, generation to generation, time and time before, pain upon pain upon pain. Shed these and create a new reality based on love.

Chapter 15

Create a Loving Reality

THIS IS WHAT ISHMEL AND I do that day: we stroll through the forest and refashion everything we had already perceived in terms of love.

We shape the trees, tall and green and firm, their pine needles shimmering perfectly. The Snake, now free of his old heavy skin, slithers down the path before us. We make the water in the lake perfectly blue, add the perfect amount of reeds on the bank, and watch as a mother duck followed by a trail of four ducklings leaves her nest to explore. We fashion the fish so they come up from below the surface to catch darting insects, making concentric ripples in the water.

We create a vibrant sunset, the first on our new world. The sun goes down in an unfolding orange splendor over the water.

We put a loving beaver family in the lake too. They set to the task of building their den, impressing all the creatures with their industrious nature. We plant many ravens in the sky, and they circle the forest with the wonderfully loud *whoo hoo* to wake the universe to the splendid magic of our awakening, perfectly synchronized with the awakening of infinity. Dusk spills through night with its millions of twinkling stars—the shooting stars are lovely as they cruise with explosive, uncontrolled intensity across the night sky, brilliant, brief, and then gone, streams of bottled intensity released quickly into the endless potential of wide-open space.

No thundershowers on this clear mountain night; instead we watch the other side of the Milky Way, clearly swooping across the night sky.

Dawn appears then with the softening of the night breezes, the rustling of alder leaves, a pink-hazed sun opening up into yellow intensity, taking over the day sky. The flowers mimic the call of the sun, budding and blooming in fast motion because we create it all in only twenty-four hours, and because everything has always been this way, because there is no such thing as time here in this place, this Eden.

We watch the Doe give birth to the twin fawns who will visit me my first night in those woods. We watch the clouds open for dozens of flying creatures, and because it is midday now and we feel especially whimsical, we create creatures that heretofore were dormant in the backs of our minds—unicorns and dragons, water nymphs and mermaids, centaurs and fairies, druids and satyrs.

You may think there could not possibly be room for all of these creatures in the forest, but the forest is laid out in such a way that it can hold a limitless amount of life, from the smallest water amoeba, floating and dividing on the lake, to the glorious sun phoenix stretching her bronzed, feathered wings the length of the sky.

It does become a bit noisy, all the chatter of this universe, and I worry it might be disturbing Peter and Sophie in their tent by the creek. To my relief, they find us in the grass by the lake and join in our creative master work. Not surprisingly, Sophie already knows Ishmel.

Ishmel lets out a thunderous roar there at the water's edge. I cower down a bit. I have forgotten just how formidable he can sound when roused. "Remember always this," he tells me, "you are both the created and the creator."

I learned that day that I have these creative channels—that everyone does—and the world we create, the way we currently live, has direct bearing on the extent to which we choose to open our own creative channeling to what we are meant to create, to our birthright, our obligation, our joy. Knowing that I am all that, I realize I have a responsibility to direct my creative energies toward the perfection that already is, has always been, and always will be, despite my prior misconceptions about the world. We will be compelled to create in the end when the world is set free from the fear that binds it, that strangles it so ruthlessly. We cannot be sustained by fear, only love, and the truth here is that when we channel that love, we find ourselves in a state of absolute bliss in and with creation.

"Did you enjoy the creating?" Ishmel asks.

"Yes, but how can it be?" I wonder.

"Remember, Darling One, whether we realize it or not, we are constantly creating, shifting energy and matter within the periphery of our own experience."

Finally, I blurt out the question that has been bothering me all along, "Who are you, Ishmel?"

"Who would you say I am?"

"I know you are my teacher . . ."

He visibly straightens at that. I can see he takes great pleasure in being my teacher.

"Are you God?"

"Yes, as are you, as are Peter and Sophie, as is the Snake, as is the Raven, as is everything. We, all of us, compose that which is holy. We, all of us, know. It is simply a matter of being aware and alive. You are God, and God is in everything around you. God is the great I Am. He is All That Is and All That Was and All That Ever Will Be."

"Ah." I jump on this one. "You said *Him*. Is God a male? As a modern woman, I have issues with that, Ishmel."

"When I refer to the Infinite Creator of All, oh Glorious Daughter, I refer to the all encompassing He/She, the universal yin/yang, so integrated, so complete that it becomes one expanding beat of love, love, love. It encompasses all of its creative and created Beloved Ones. If you feel a pull from inside, a desire to make something, be something, sing something, know that your urge comes from God."

"But what about ego?" I feel bold now in questioning Ishmel, as though I can ask him anything. "How do I know when I am guided, that it is not just my ego, my small-minded, singular self trying to have her way, trying to hoard more than I need?"

"More of what, Darling One? For what do you tend to grasp?"

I feel uncomfortable and shift my position in the grass. "For me it is not so much things I crave as attention—glory, fame, I suppose."

"You are extremely brave to admit your temptation. There are several main temptations that appeal to human individuals, and we can discuss those if you like. For now, know that the way to determine if your urgings are driven by the great As Is involves sensing whether the basic vibration of what you are feeling is love. Creative urges prompted by love have a distinct sensation that you will learn to recognize. It feels like light. It feels like peace. When you move with the love tone, you will know you are correct because there will be no conflict, within or without, as you move."

"So many times, I question my love urgings because they seem a bit crazy, like coming out here to meet you, for instance. I'm scared my imagination is getting the better of my ability to reason."

"Know this: You do not come to God through reason or logic. The way to God is through imagination. Imagination is different from imaginary. Imagination is not crazy or pretend or made up, and it is never scared. Instead, imagination is wide open to the possibilities of love."

In retrospect, I believe it is not so much that Ishmel and I created a universe with animals and creatures devised by us as it is that we shed the mask that covered our vision of that universe. We re-created our vision, and now we see Life, the world, our world, as it is—perfect, absolutely perfect—and that alone is reason for celebration.

I sit there at the lake with Ishmel and Sophie while Peter takes pictures of the animals and plants around us—*snap, snap, snap* goes the shutter of his camera. I think about God and imagination. I begin to see God as the creator of all creators—writer, dancer, painter, singer, lover, chef, gardener, architect, designer, photographer, producer, the penultimate artist, the absolute alive, ever-morphing, ever-creating, joyful, artist's artist. As I sit there, I know I will never go back to my ordinary life. I vow to stay in communion with Ishmel and the plants and animals of the forest, with Sophie and Peter, forever, and because there is no time, that would be nothing, a flash of wonder, and an infinite stretch of eternity all at once.

I lean pleasantly into the damp grass and completely surrender to the oneness of creation around, under, above, and through me. I look out at that vast blue sky and focus on clouds drifting by in various shapes, huge, bear-like fluffs, relatives of Ishmel, the Raven, the Spider, the Snake, the animal characters from my lovely drama spin around me in the threads of the clouds. I enjoy the show because I know that it is both specific and special to me and stunning and applicable to all of creation at the same time. I love that.

Now comes the sound of drummers. I sit straight up at the noise, but Ishmel, Sophie, and Peter do not react. Evidently the drumming has been happening all through the night and into this new day. How could I have missed it?

Tum, tum, tum—the sound is steady and grounding and sure. I turn toward the lodge and see them—a row of women beating out their steady, sure sound into the beauty of dawn. They sit at the picnic bench, six of them, all beautiful. The lead drummer at the front of the row holds her huge side drum with her knees. Her red hair flows down her shoulders and catches the drift of wind swirling around all of us; strands of red hair float hypnotically into space as she strikes the drum rhythmically with sticks. One in the middle with a solid, curvy frame, her blond hair cut in a thick bob, pieces of it catching the rising sun until she glows, a beam of sun herself. She *tap, tap, taps* on the top of her drum, synchronizing the sound perfectly with the lead woman. Another woman, a bit shorter than the other two, her hair curling every which way, a reflection of her own playfulness, her eyes the brightest blue as if bits of that perfect sky had planted themselves into her being, rings a bell at the end of each stanza.

The drumming continues quite steadily now, and I recognize the pattern of their drumbeat from before. I'd been hearing it often in these woods in my subconscious mind, steadied by its regularity. I'd even heard that *tum, tum, tum* in Los Angeles. Their sound, their lovely beat, followed me home last year, but I missed it somehow.

Now the dancers appear. They twirl in bright flowing skirts over the grass to the rhythm of the drumbeat. They are light and airy, with bracelets on their arms and ankles. Every once in a while, the bracelets clink together with a pleasant, seductive sound as the dancers turn.

Ishmel smiles at me. He saw them all along, and at last I too am aware of them in that space. The joy of their dance overtakes me, and I lift myself up from the grass and twirl with them. Carried by the wind and the drums and the harmonizing sounds of the birds, I float in circles on that lawn. I am free and sexy and alive. It feels wonderful.

Only now, as I became aware of the drummers and the dancers with their perpetual rhythm, do I notice the other people in the lodge. They are dressed in loose-fitting clothes in various colors—blacks and oranges, yellows, greens, and reds. When I look through the large glass window facing the lake, I see that they are doing yoga: triangle pose, warrior, headstands, splits. Some hang on the back wall from ropes. Some lay on mats doing leg stretches. The elk head over the fireplace beams down at the yogis, evidently happy for their presence. They move, sway, and stretch.

I notice something else I'd never seen before. I see their auras, lovely and colorful, beaming out from their bodies at all seven chakra points or energy centers. Over the crowns of their heads shines the brilliant, pure light of consciousness, clear and dazzling. The yogis resemble angels, but I realize they are indeed human, of this earth, communing with the earth.

For an instant, I think I see Ishmel in that room. He is a man under the elk's head leading the group. I recognize the flowing black hair and clear blue eyes. Yes, it *is* Ishmel. He moves with the rhythm of the drums, as does everyone in that room. I pause in wonderment. Can Ishmel be in two places at the same time? I am instantaneously dazzled and confused and, for a split second, I suspect that Ishmel is all of the people in that room at once. Was he also present in the drummers and the dancers on the lawn? I turn quickly toward the Bear and, in a flash of recognition, I see him in the trees and grass, on the lake, and in every part of the world we have created together. I look back at the window again, this time at my own reflection, and realize there are bits of Ishmel in me too. He is Everywhere. Everywhere is part of him. There is no separation, and I feel peaceful and excited by this prospect.

Everything glitters in an odd way just then, as if one of the shiniest stars from the evening sky has split into millions of tiny pieces and scattered itself to make all of us. I feel dizzy. I reach toward Ishmel the Bear, perhaps he might steady me, but I am not fast enough.

Without warning, an ear-shattering, harsh *bang* of gunshot blasts across the peace of that moment. Ishmel crumples to the ground.

Chapter 16

Illusions

So it is that Ishmel, the embodiment of the Bear, passes before my eyes, and Brian, the man I have chosen to marry, to live with as my husband, has fired the shot that ushers Ishmel from my presence.

I fling my body over the Bear's corpse. Bitter tears fall, but they are more from shock than absorption of the complete extent of my loss, of the loss to Everyone in that lovely dream that is our mutual creation. All the creatures on that lawn freeze in the same silent shock at the shotgun's blast.

Quickly, my shock transforms to grief. It is as if my insides are wrenched from my body, as if the burning in my heart that had ignited with love freezes into ice.

I look toward Brian and his still-smoking weapon in utter confusion. Brian drops the gun. I recognize a mixture of grief and shame in his eyes. My mouth forms the one word that comes into my mind at that point, "Why?"

Brian shakes his head, takes one step away from me, and flees into the woods.

It had been easy, suspiciously easy, to believe and follow Ishmel's precepts when I was there in that lovely forest alone with him, when everything was beautiful and innocent and safe. It is quite another thing to stick to the precepts when the master, the one who taught them, lies prone, dead at my feet.

The precepts flip through my brain like cards on the flip charts movie directors use to lay out scenes:

1. All your needs will be met.

No, I argue within myself as I run my fingers through Ishmel's bloodied fur. I long for him, and he is physically gone forever. As I look up the path by the lake where Brian sprinted away, I know that no new Ishmel will appear in the flesh to comfort me. There is only my own mind, alone, lost, abandoned. It's an ugly feeling, that of abandonment. A sense of absolute betrayal courses through me. How dare he? Teach me to relax, that all my needs will be met, and then let himself be ripped violently away from me, leaving me raw and confused and cut off from the only person I ever really needed: him. "Ishmel, Ishmel. You have forsaken me without warning, with no preparation. How can I possibly survive under these conditions?"

It occurs to me that Ishmel's departure wasn't planned at all. Why bother to believe in a divine plan at this point? Ishmel's death looks random. If it is random, isn't all of the rest of life random also? *All your needs will be met* sounds like a cosmic joke, my security seems little more secure than betting on a certain number in the roll of dice.

2. Time is an illusion.

In my supreme anger, I scoff at Precept Two. There had been a time when Ishmel lived, and there is now a time after his death, a before and an after, a clear dividing line. I touch his body and feel the remnants of living warmth escape Ishmel's dead shell. I focus on the past, my time with Ishmel, and despair at my future, long stretches of existence without him. There is only the past or the future in my mind; the present disappears altogether. time rushes in to take its position at the throne of being since now, that gap, that cosmic placeholder between what has happened and what will happen, is removed.

3. No fear.

I shiver now, and Sophie, a psychologist by trade, wraps a blanket around my shoulders. I startle, look in her eyes, and begin to suspect she is humoring me as part of some psychological experiment. Maybe she and Peter laugh at me in the privacy of their tent late at night. I could be their case study in craziness, in failure. Yes, that's what is happening. I push the blanket away. "Fuck off!" I yell at her.

Her eyes cloud with hurt confusion.

Good, I tell myself. She'll think twice before making me the butt of her jokes again.

The dancers speak in hushed tones, and I stand to face them all. But now they don't look lovely at all. They are demons with burning yellow eyes and twisted black wings. Their only purpose is to torment me.

I scream and back away from them all. The Raven circles above with her *whoo hoo*. I recognize her for what she is: a portent of hell.

4. Release into Love.

How can I release into the supposed love of such beings? All I perceive now is demonic and frightening. My terror of the others bounces off the violence I have watched Brian commit, and it boomerangs into a nasty sludge over everyone and everything else. I myself stiffen from within. My stomach clenches into a tight knot.

I do not trust these others at all, so separate, so threatening, so foreign from myself. Ishmel was my guru. They have nothing to do with him, and now he is gone, torn from me through no fault of mine. Everyone else is to blame. Were Brian, the chief perpetrator of Ishmel's death, present, I would rip him apart, take his gun, and use it first on him and then on myself.

5. Create a loving reality.

Ishmel's body grows cold before me. How am I to see his crumpled, lifeless form as an illusion? I can reach out and touch it. I know with all logic and reason that Ishmel will no longer be around to advise and comfort me. My former sense that I can assist in the creation of beauty and perfection completely vanishes. The beings looking at me with their strange, demon eyes are neither beautiful nor perfect.

Sophie and Peter reach out to me, but I only see them as menacing, coming straight for Ishmel's body. The other demons on the lawn crowd toward me. I am trapped, the center of a circle where scary beings with even scarier motives come toward me.

I scream. The trees around us reverberate with my horror. When I look up at their shaking leaves, I suspect the trees are just as menacing as the people. What is this place where I have come? I am stuck here, stranded, with no chance of returning to my prior life. How can I ever be the same?

Who was Ishmel anyway? Just another one of them, was he not? What has he really done for me? Suddenly, I don't feel enlightened or peaceful. I feel confused. Maybe Brian was right to destroy him. Maybe Brian knows the truth and has saved me. But I can never be entirely with Brian because I can never completely let go of Ishmel.

I back away from Ishmel's bloody body and make my way through a gap in the circle.

"Come," Sophie beckons. "Be with us."

I look at her moist eyes and the scene of desperate sorrow on the lawn.

"No," I shout at all of them. "No, no, no, no!"

Chapter 17

PRECEPT SIX:

Connect Energy Lines to Heal the World

WHERE DO WE GO WHEN our entire concept of the universe completely shatters? I thought I was so strong, firm in my belief in the precepts. Now I am unsure of Ishmel himself. The sky becomes dark and ominous. I run.

I run past my tent, past the rock formation, past all that is familiar, deep into the forest. I want to be lost, to get away from my created world that now seems a sham. I want to escape the growing sense that all my supposed moves toward enlightenment were bullshit.

I stumble over stray branches and fall with a soft thud onto the dry pine needles at my feet. Thunder claps as the afternoon showers begin. Usually the afternoon rain is a soothing refreshment in the summer heat, but now it seems sinister and unforgiving. Rain soaks through my clothes, blowing cruelly into my eyes, and I continue stumbling through the woods.

I trip a second time, and twigs scratch my arms. As I scramble on the forest floor, pine needles blow into both my eyes. I scream in anguish and sink to the ground.

I am nothing, have nothing, can be nothing. No one cares if I crumple up and die here. I sob and feel the blood from my eyes roll down my cheeks, mixing with the rain on the bed of pine needles below me.

"Oh my God." It is Brian's voice I hear now. "What's happened to you?"

"Go away. Get away from me!" I shout toward him.

"It's all my fault." His voice is low, confessional. "That bear wasn't usual, was he?"

There is a rustle from the top of an alder tree next to us. Brian draws in his breath.

"What do you see?" I demand.

"An Eagle." More rustling from above. "It's gigantic," Brian says.

I stand. I feel the whoosh of wings right next to my face.

"Brian?"

"Sorry. Yes, it's right here. You don't suppose it might attack? Maybe we should take cover or something."

But there is no time for that. The Eagle swoops closer, and I feel her talons on my shoulder, and then I hear her voice, soft, steady, and majestic. "You must connect, My Dear. Find a connection," she says.

"A connection? What sort of connection?"

"Who are you talking to?" Brian's voice sounds weak.

"The Eagle," I whisper.

"Of course." He sounds worried.

"You can't hear her?" I ask. "Not even a bit?"

"No." I sense his extreme disappointment.

The Eagle continues. "Let your anger melt into love."

"It's not that simple," I protest.

"But it is, My Child. It is simply a matter of courage."

The Eagle releases my shoulders and flies to perch on a branch above us. Brian sits beside me in what is now pouring rain. He holds my hand.

"Your father's taken a bad turn," he offers. "That's why I came in the first place. I didn't mean . . . I'm sorry about the bear. I thought he was attacking you."

I cry bitter tears now for the loss of everything, for Ishmel, for Brian and me as we were before, as we can never be again. That is when the Eagle flies down again and whispers in my ear.

"Look to the obvious about where you are, and who stands beside you. The obvious lends itself to the non-judgmental, to an open mind. Open your mind to accept the man at your side," she says. "Comfort him and learn compassion."

"I don't want to have compassion for him," I counter. "He killed Ishmel."

"You yourself know it is quite impossible to kill the Grizzly."

"But he's gone."

"Use your energy, your strong life current to call to him anytime you like, and he will come. Summon him and the others."

"I don't want others," I argue. "I came into these woods to get away from people and their problems. In L.A., I'm surrounded by humanity. Why would I send out my precious energy, this love energy that's taken me two years to cultivate, to anyone else? It's not their business."

The Eagle laughs. "Because otherwise it will wither away and become quite impotent. You can't keep love in a box."

I am silent. The Eagle stays nearby on the forest floor. "You must turn to compassion," she finally advises. "Compassion for yourself. Compassion for this man. Compassion for Everyone. Return to the light. See the truth that is you."

I turn, furious, to face her voice. I grope, blindly with my hands in her direction.

"I can't see anything," I insist. "This is nuts. How do I know I'm even talking to you? Brian can't hear you—"

"Actually," Brian interrupts, "there is a kind of murmur now."

I shake my head. "Now you tell me you can hear the words." "Well, not entirely." He is apologetic. "But I think there may be something interesting going on here."

The Eagle continues, loud, clear, and undeniable, "Feel free, feel His vibe, and we will heal the world."

I turn to her. "Look, I'm not smart enough to do what you're asking, feel his vibe and heal the world. The whole world? That's a big place." I sigh. "Maybe I don't want to see anymore. He kept telling me time is an illusion, a fake, and if that were true, then he can't have died, but he did. He left me all alone."

"He will never leave you," the Eagle declares. "Have you so quickly forgotten the lesson of the Snake? Are you not yourself a creature of this forest as well as the city?"

Salty tears well up in my eyes. She is right. I am both part of this forest and part of Los Angeles. Temporal and transcendent at once, as was Ishmel.

As I cry, my sight returns. I realize the wounds from the pine needles were not permanent. I can heal, and as my eyes heal, bits of my skeptical spirit, that which holds me back, heal also. My tears cleanse in the sense that they make everything clear again. I look out at the world around me and see that everything in it sparkles. Bits of spare raindrops sparkle from the leaves. The grass sparkles. The Eagle's wings glisten in the sunlight that breaks through the clouds, through what had seemed utter darkness beforehand.

The Eagle takes flight at that moment. She soars with a whoosh up past the tops of the pine trees and into the still, cloud-streaked sky, misty from the rain. She forms a giant arch in the sky, and as she moves, lovely colors, hues of every variety, swirl out beneath her wings. They group together in that misty sky to form a rainbow. Brian takes my hand, and I let him. I realize his eyes are also moist. We stand there together, hand in hand, and watch the rainbow shimmer in the sky.

A feeling of peace hits me after I see the rainbow. I have a satisfied sense that Ishmel is actually nearby, as is everything and everyone lovely, and created by me. I sigh and release Brian's hand.

"The bear," Brian says. "I shot him because I thought he was coming at you. I was worried you might get hurt." An awkward silence between us. "I'm sorry," he finally finishes.

"You were protecting me in your mind. Don't be sorry. I understand." I take his hand and open myself to what Brian has to offer, to what the forest has to offer, to Life itself.

"I love you," Brian declares.

"I love you too," I say, and I mean it.

Chapter 18

Butterflies in Los Angeles

• *November 13, 2009*

I'm living out the fall exclusively in Los Angeles. I live here because it is where Brian has his work.

Our backyard in Santa Monica is inundated with butterflies. Before then, they crawled through our small, city plot of grass as caterpillars in various shades. Now they transform and float around the yard; they change from base creatures of the soil into air creatures—lovely, delicate, and true.

I can't pinpoint the exact moment of my own transformation. It's been gradual. My physical looks remain fairly similar to who I was before the change, although I did grow out my hair. I stand a bit taller. My transformation is not so much physical as that of the butterflies, although I hear from other people that I glow more. I repeat the mantra "yes" often to myself. I say yes to pain, yes to awareness, yes to love when it is offered to me, yes to all of it.

Although I've transformed in the city with Brian, I've become restless with my decision to stay here. Brian loves me as a mortal man loves a woman, and in our relationship, I am often reminded of my parents. Brian is easy to live with because I love him without obsession. I've kept the forest within me, and keep listing the Six Precepts for living over and over again:

1. *All your needs will be met.*
2. *Time is an illusion.*
3. *No fear.*
4. *Release into love.*
5. *Create a loving reality.*
6. *Connect energy lines to heal the world.*

I suspect there is a Seventh Precept, one that it has something to do with finding peace in the world with all the pain and joy that involves being human. I'd like to know what that is.

I wish I could tell you that my life is perfect with Brian, but I cannot. We quarrel occasionally.

I've discovered I am pregnant. I know I must leave Brian and return to those woods to answer my "Who am I?" question and find Ishmel.

• *December 8, 2009*

I must deal with the physical decline of my father. Last week, he discovered his cancer is inoperable, and we've started hearing a Coyote howl in our backyard. As always, the Coyote's howl is piercing and unnerving. There was a drought last summer in Southern California, and lots of animals from Topanga Canyon come down into Santa Monica, where we live, for water. None of the neighbors can actually see the Coyote, but we all hear him. His howl always sounds like it is directly in the backyard, but whenever anyone goes outside to find him, they realize the howl originates somewhere else, someplace quite unidentifiable because his howl echoes everywhere. Brian called animal control, but they haven't managed to catch this particular Coyote. As usual, he is tricky and elusive.

I wait every night for the sound of Coyote, the trickster. His howl echoes into my pregnant belly, giving my baby and my life a whirl. I really miss the forest—ache for it, actually. I know the Coyote's call came from it. Sometimes I walk the streets around Cedars-Sinai Medical Center after visiting my dad in intensive care, and think about that howl.

Sometimes I return home and sit silently, hoping Ishmel will come into my mind with the missing precept about healing and connecting and joy. He never does.

My father becomes sicker and sicker, and I find myself making decisions for him that I never wanted to make—nursing homes, care facilities, and hospices.

My mother, tired, aging before my eyes. Brian, understanding, but constantly gone at his work. Brian's workaholic tendencies take a new turn now that I am pregnant. His worries multiply. How will we support this baby? He sees himself in an old-fashioned sense as the man, the provider for our household. I fall into the pattern with a sense of relief. I plan to stay home with the baby. She is a daughter, this new person in my belly. I know it before the ultrasound confirms the fact. A girl, my daughter is coming.

I visit my father more and more often. Each time, I resolve to mention the precepts from the forest to him. I suspect he will be interested in the idea of time being an illusion. He should know that his imminent death is not death at all, that if he chooses, he can remain in contact with all of us. I long to tell my father about Ishmel and that he can be contacted telepathically. I know that I can shoot energy, my healing energy, into my father and sustain him. Sometimes I do just that. I shoot my dad energy without saying a word. I sit there silently and direct the healing light from my body into his. He lies there on his sick bed, and I know he feels it.

My father is in all respects a practical man. He remains that way now. Instead of discussions of healing and transformation, we talk about money. Dad tells me about his 401(k) plan and how I am to withdraw certain amounts from it to care for my mother after he leaves. He explains interest rates and stock options. He becomes supremely annoyed when I lose interest in this topic. "What kind of a daughter are you?" he laments. "One of those helpless women who don't know about their funds?" Money is the be-all and end-all for him. He so wants me to get money, to be good with money, but I lack the skills. Again and again, I disappoint him.

There is no question that he will die soon. A Roman Catholic by birth and an atheist throughout life, my father deflects any discussion of the spiritual portents of his exit. I don't bring it up.

• *December 30, 2009*

I am six months pregnant now. My father knows he will never see his granddaughter.

The night he leaves, I sit at his bedside. My mother is home asleep. Dad turns to me and makes the most intimate comment he can manage. "I like having you around," he says.

I take a risk at this point. I know it is now or never. "I love you, Dad," I tell him. He turns away. It is too much for him, of course, my statement of love. I know he cannot return it, but I say it again anyway. "I never said that enough when I was growing up. I love you, Dad. I love you."

And that is when he extends his hand to me and knows who I am. He forgives me with his eyes for who I am. Then he turns his head from me and passes away. In one moment, he is in his body, and in the next, he is gone. It is that simple.

Chapter 19

PRECEPT SEVEN:

Vibrate with Joy

I ARRANGE FOR THE BURIAL of my dad, a man with intense passion with whom I have never quite been able to connect. I tend to my mother, who goes into shock at Dad's departure. I cash the retirement savings in amortized bits as my father instructed. He is that type of a man, my father. He didn't want Mom to exhaust their funds too soon.

My daughter grows and grows inside me, and I glow from my impending motherhood, the most basic of creative pursuits. At the same time, I long for the forest.

I loathe the thought of raising her in Los Angeles, so I book a flight to northern Montana for January. It is thirteen degrees in Helena, possibly colder in the mountains. Brian throws a fit. I promise to stay inside this time, in Sophie and Peter's cabin next to that same forest where I first spotted Ishmel. Peter is in residence there photographing for *National Geographic*.

On some level, I suspect Brian worries I will leave him for good this time, and I suppose he is justified in this fear. I contemplate taking up residence permanently in a cabin like Sophie and Peter have and living quietly off the sizable inheritance my father left me.

I'd have time then to consider who I am, and to find the resolution to the story. I want to record the Six Precepts and to discover the Seventh Precept I know must exist. The precepts, though personal to me, are meant for you also.

As for the Sixth Precept—connect the energy lines between all living things, and heal the world—perhaps as I discover I am capable of this healing, that my very attitude can alter my environment and the lives of others, you too will uncover this power. Perhaps it is everyone's purpose to some extent, to heal the world from its poisons, the toxins that begin in the mind.

• *January 4, 2010*

I arrived in Montana today, seven months pregnant, bleary eyed about the loss of my father. The forest is frozen, lifeless. There were no drummers or twirling dancers from the summer. Peter picked me up at the airport and drove me to their cabin where Sophie had prepared a warming vegetable stew. They've also prepared a guest room, complete with a fireplace, for me.

"Any news of the Bear?" I get to the point after a preliminary discussion of inclement weather and my upcoming role as a mother.

Peter and Sophie exchange a look. "There has been no physical contact," Sophie informs me.

Sophie makes sure I am considerably bundled: long underwear, scarf, hat, several layers of sweaters, and a thick down jacket before she agrees to let me take the short mile walk around the lake. "Only because the sun is shining," she says.

I seek Ishmel in the flesh. I suspect it is a pipe dream because the last time I saw the Grizzly, he was laid out on the grass with a fatal gunshot wound.

I am visited by a Doe. I am not sure if it is the same deer from three summers ago or one of the fawns grown up with her own family. She sleeps outside our cabin all night. When I exit in the morning, she crouches in the grass and looks at me with huge loving eyes. She is a spirit goddess of the woods. She moves softly through the grass around the cabin, and in the absence of Ishmel's all-encompassing power, she comforts me. She is lovely and strong.

Still no Ishmel. I always knew he was my teacher, from the first moment I sensed him following me in these woods. What I didn't expect was how much I would love him. I force myself to relax. I listen to the soft wind all around me, the Doe's footsteps—soft, soft, soft on the pine needles.

I surrender to the warmth of the sun on my back through the thick layers of sweaters and Sophie's coat, to the soft vibrancy of the pine and alder trees reflecting off the silent lake. I let go of any remnants of the old stale environment from my life before the precepts. I surrender to joy. As I do this, I open up to the limitless possibilities of reaching Ishmel. I find myself supercharged with potential, and then it happens. My imagination takes flight with my intention, and in that instant, I realize Ishmel is always there inside me. He has never left. There was never was any separation in the first place. The Ishmel within cannot be killed. He is always alive, beating in the very heart of me. My body seems to hum.

I know true healing is possible because in a sense there is never anything to heal in the first place, because we are never separate. God is love. God is powerful. There is no problem God cannot solve. You are the way, the truth, and the light, and there is no way to reach the Father, the Divine Infinite, but through the love link in your own heart. Once you know that secret—the grand, overflowing thousand-petalled lotus that never stops blooming in you, in all of us—we will heal the world.

Once I allow myself to be surprised by this joy, I contact Ishmel. I don't expect anything that day as I trudge around the lake in the snow. It is thirty-five degrees, freezing for an Angeleno. I wonder what happened to all the people from before. I regret my behavior the day Ishmel was shot—the way I fled into the forest, oblivious of the Others. Had they suffered also at the physical loss of the Bear? How quickly I sprang into disbelief upon that loss—even as I felt his presence all around me, I denied it. I chose to not believe. Why?

As I walk the short lake path, I question the wisdom of this winter trip. I wonder about Brian and my mother back in Los Angeles. I am due to return in a few days for a doctor's check-up on my growing daughter. It is then I notice a colorful tepee across the lake. It is large and lovely with brightly colored designs painted on its surface. Who lives there? Is it a Blackfoot Indian left from generations before? Is it someone I have yet to meet who visits only in the winter? Aren't they cold out here, in their tepee in the snow?

I follow the path toward the tepee. "Hello?" I announce myself at the entrance. When there is no answer, I poke my head through the open flaps that make up the door.

It is empty inside. There is a chair and a table. In the corner on elevated slats is a sleeping bag. The inside of the tepee feels delightfully warm. It is as if an unseen fire burns from its center. Odd, this warmth, I think, particularly since the hole in the top is open to the crystal-blue winter sky. I can't resist. I step inside, and tie the flaps shut with the rope there to block any cold air from outside.

I sit down in the chair and, bit by bit, shed layers of clothing. Eventually I am down to only my jeans and a thin T-shirt. I lean back in the chair that is amazingly cozy. I relax. I become so relaxed, I let go of all my prior misgivings about this trip. This is the perfect place for me to be, quite natural.

I let my eyes close and become aware of a soft glow near me; something crouches at the edge of the tepee. How did I miss this something or someone when I entered?

My eyes flick open to see the Bear himself, Ishmel, in all his grandeur. I see the hole where the gunshot wound must have entered his heart, but it is only incidental to his living, glowing presence. He is alive and well and himself.

"Ishmel?" I whisper, and in that instant, he transforms into a man, muscular with long black hair in a knot at the nape of his neck, blue eyes glowing. He reaches out his arms, and I gladly let him cradle me. I am so tired then, too tired. I lean into the muscles of his chest, and he holds me in silence for a long while. Eventually, I drift off into the deepest, most comforting, most refreshing sleep imaginable, knowing in my heart that everything is okay, that it has always been okay, and that now that I am in his home, I too will be eternally well.

Chapter 20

The Rapture of the Yogis

IT IS SOPHIE WHO WAKES me from my sleep. When she does, Ishmel is gone. At first, she suspected I froze to death in that tepee, but when she approached, she saw my breath. She touches my arm, and I sit straight up as from a dream.

"I saw Him," I tell her in absolute ecstasy. "He was just here."

She embraces me at that. For a while we both sit, still and glowing together. The tepee remains surprisingly warm; the invisible fire smolders away at its center.

"Is this His house?" I venture.

"No," Sophie corrects. "Emily lives here. Do you know Emily?"

"I don't think so."

"But you met her last summer. She's one of the yogis here in residence."

I remember that day I pressed my nose against the glass of the lodge window, convinced at first that everyone there was a derivation of Ishmel, that He had multiplied. Then later, I was sure they were all demons, come to torment me. I lower my head in embarrassment at my remembrance of my behavior. It did look then like Ishmel was dead, but of course, that was impossible.

Sophie takes my hand, and we both stand. "Why not meet them all again? Emily and the others."

"I have to leave in two days."

"But they're here now. They're always here," she counters. Even as we exit the tepee, I see their movements through the window across the lake. "Peter's there today. Taking photographs."

We quickly make our way along the path to the lodge. I can hear the music coming from that room: joyful, pounding, hypnotic.

Sophie and I enter through the back. I hope to sneak in unnoticed, but a woman with the broadest, loveliest smile in the universe rushes toward me for a hug. In an instant, I recognize her. She is one of the drummers from the summer, and she is also oddly familiar from someplace else. Then it hits me. She works with Brian at the studio back in Los Angeles. She is always open and friendly and smiling there too. Emily: she has been around me all along.

Now all the other yogis surround me, commenting on how cute I look in my pregnancy and giving me hugs. I realize they are all familiar from my daily life in Los Angeles: the man who works at the dry cleaner, the receptionist at the school where I work, colleagues whom Brian and I love and admire. These are the people from all around me; they shower me with support. I haven't recognized it, or them, until just now.

"You must be angels from Heaven." I tremble.

Emily laughs. "But you're already there. Heaven's right here, right now, with you all the time. There are simply those who perceive it, and those who don't know."

"I saw Ishmel today," I murmur.

"So have we all. He is always with us."

I glance toward the front of the room, under the elk's head, and yes, there is Ishmel the man, looking quite the same as He had earlier in Emily's tent. He has the same lovely glow about Him, and I realize that He is the source of the invisible fire in this room as He had been in Emily's tent.

As I continue focusing on Him, the light surrounding Him becomes so bright as to be blinding, like when you stare at the midday sun for too long. The light reflects through and off Him, out to Everyone, and then I become aware that all the others in that room are beaming their own light and warmth also.

The whole room pulsates with Joy. I feel a tingling sensation throughout my body, and when I look at my hands and feet, I realize that I emanate the same intense light as Everyone Else. I glance one more time to the front of the room, to Ishmel, and witness something I have long suspected is possible. He disappears. In one instant He is there leading the group, and in the next, there is nothing in that space at all. All of Ishmel, none of Ishmel, there and not there, instantaneously.

Now I realize that Everyone in the room is doing the same. One by one, they radiate a bright, intense light and then disappear. There is always a moment, a flash when they are two places at once, here in the lodge, and Somewhere Else.

I find myself alone, the last one standing in that room. I think about them: Ishmel, Sophie, Peter, Emily, Everyone there in that sacred space. I acknowledge just how special, how gifted, and how intelligent they all are, that they embody God in their individual living, that they are each gifts to me personally, and to the entire universe. I beam my thankfulness for them out into infinity. I celebrate the change in my perception of them, wowed by the instantaneous change of my perception from something toxic into Love. I sink deeper and deeper into the feeling of Love until—*flash*—I disappear. I am there in the lodge and Somewhere Else at the same time. I disappear and reappear—again and again and again.

- *Every Day Now*

There are all sorts of reasons why I seek Ishmel. I listen for Him sometimes because I enjoy His largeness, the wonder and power of His being. Other times, I turn to Him for comfort—His voice is by turns soothing and serious and soft. More and more, I turn to Him when I feel lost. He comes to me when I feel trammeled by humanity or when I feel abandoned by them. I can hear Him in city malls and traffic jams; He fills the empty spaces of time where I feel lonely and deserted and by myself. To actually see Him embodied is shocking and wonderful but rare. Usually what happens is He enters through the seed He planted in my heart. The seed is multifaceted and potent. It aches when I neglect it, but when I give it the proper attention, it flourishes and blooms until it fills my heart with loveliness. That's when I fall to my knees from the joy of it all and let my heart beat with "Thank you, thank you, thank you." I like those times.

About the Author

LAURA CARPINI graduated magna cum laude in English literature from UCLA. After a brief career as an attorney, she became a middle school teacher. In addition to this book, she has written several screenplays and is already at work on a sequel to *Bear Speaks*. She is an active yogi and lives in Los Angeles with her husband and daughter.

To Our Readers

WEISER BOOKS, AN IMPRINT OF Red Wheel/Weiser, publishes books across the entire spectrum of occult and esoteric subjects. Our mission is to publish quality books that will make a difference in people's lives without advocating any one particular path or field of study. We value the integrity, originality, and depth of knowledge of our authors.

Our readers are our most important resource, and we appreciate your input, suggestions, and ideas about what you would like to see published. Please feel free to contact us to request our latest book catalog, or to be added to our mailing list.

Red Wheel/Weiser, LLC
500 Third Street, Suite 230
San Francisco, CA 94107
www.redwheelweiser.com

Discussion Questions

1. The protagonist has a wobbly relationship with her father. To what extent does he influence her, and provide her with the skills that allow her to expand her perception of the world in the forest? What is the general role of family in the story?

2. The main character's initial reason for going to the forest is to prove her independence. Yet, from the beginning, she is reliant on Jerry, handyman and forest ranger extraordinaire. How are her interactions with him a precursor for discoveries about herself and independence that she has later in the story?

3. How does the appearance of the Coyote become a turning point in the woman's interactions with the forest? How does her relationship with him help her settle into her environment?

4. Discuss the earthquake and Ishmel's entrance. How does her initial perception of the Bear as a "stalker" contribute to her fear and excitement when they finally make contact?

5. Discuss the significance of the name Ishmel. What does the Bear's name reveal about what she will learn from him?

6. The woman finds herself drawn to both the Grizzly and Brian. What is the basis for her attraction to Brian, and how does it differ from her need for Ishmel?

7. The protagonist toys many times with leaving the forest. What direct evidence does she have for the veracity of her experience with the Grizzly, and what finally convinces her to stay?

8. What are some of the elements of shamanism in the story? To what extent does the main character become a shaman herself?

9. How does the woman's experience with the Spider affect the way she sees her own survival in light of the precepts? To what extent does that survival depend on her ability to release into love?

10. The woman describes Peter and Sophie as "the epitome of the married couple." How do they foil her relationship with Brian, and the tension she often feels there?

11. How does Brian cope with the protagonist's withdrawal from him into nature? What do their arguments about camping reveal about their relationship?

12. When the woman first meets Sherry she sees her as a rival for Ishmel's affections. What does that jealousy show her about her feelings toward the Bear, and how does her view of Sherry change when she gets more information?

13. What is the lesson of the Woman in the Cave? Why does the woman warn the protagonist about Ishmel? Are those warnings legitimate?

14. There are several points in the story where the woman doesn't see Ishmel physically, and feels abandoned. What events show her that he is always with her, and how does that discovery tie in with his teaching that time and space are mental constructs?

15. What does the protagonist learn about the role fear plays in her development? How does confronting her fear help her evolve as an individual, and ultimately allow her to become part of a community?

16. Consider how each of the precepts prompts the main character's psychological evolution. Compare her personality at the beginning of the story with who she becomes in the end.

17. Discuss the two rainstorms in the story and the main character's reactions to them. How do the Snake's movements in the second storm coincide with her internal opening? How does that internal change allow her to refashion the external appearance of the forest?

18. Discuss the protagonist's pregnancy and how it connects with Ishmel's teaching about immortality and the ongoing nature of life.

19. To what extent is it necessary to retreat into nature and leave one's ordinary surroundings to develop as a human being? Is it possible to get in touch with Truth while living in a city, and continuing to fulfill the daily requirements of a family and job? How would you imagine that happening?

20. Ishmel's precepts serve as a bridge between the protagonist and God. This connection shifts her perception, leading her to a place of joy. Can you imagine using these precepts to change your perception of what is happening in the world? Discuss.